Resort

#2 in the Gra

Jam

Resort to Murder
Grant's Crossing Series
Book #2
Copyright © 2022 by Jamie Tremain
FIRST EDITION
Published January 31 2022

For more information, address: jamietremainJT@yahoo.com

www.jamietremain.ca[1]
Cover Design by Jennifer Gibson – www.JenniferGibson.ca[2]

---

1. http://www.billeelliotauthor.com

2. http://www.JenniferGibson.ca

Also by Jamie Tremain

Dorothy Dennehy Mystery Series
The Silk Shroud
Lightning Strike
Beholden to None

Grant's Crossing
Grant's Crossing - Death on the Alder
Resort to Murder

Watch for more at www.jamietremain.ca.

Table of Contents

Acknowledgements

We'd like to thank Linda Melnyk, and Carol Grey for suggesting Roxy and Ryker, respectively, as names for the two crias born in this book.

And huge thanks to our beta readers for their invaluable feedback and suggestions – Carol, Gloria, Michele, and Rebecca.

CHAPTER ONE
Alysha

"Look at this, Alysha! They've found a body on the grounds of the new spa!"

I'd been enjoying a peaceful breakfast with my partner, Jeff Iverson, contemplating the day ahead of me. My thoughts came to an abrupt halt when he rustled our local morning paper in front of my face.

"It says here that one of the servers at the restaurant was killed after the premises closed last night. His body was discovered after an anonymous phone call. The police are not commenting on their investigation. And everything there is closed until further notice." He laid the paper down and pretended to sulk. "So, there goes our couples' massage you promised me, at least until it opens again."

I pulled the paper towards me and shuddered at the headlines. A suspicious death had been my welcome when I returned to Grant's Crossing just over a year ago. Deja vu chills ran down my arms. "Not again? This is too close to home. Give me a minute to regroup, babe."

I pushed away from the table and walked out onto our small balcony.

Most days Jeff and I enjoyed breakfast in the dining room with the other Leven Lodge residents where we lived, but this morning we'd decided to have a private first meal of the day in our own space. And it had been peaceful until he had read the local paper.

I had inherited Leven Lodge the previous year from my Uncle Dalton Grant. My family, the Grants, had owned this property, and the nearby sawmill, for many years. The will's conditions stipulated that I'd be taking on active seniors to live out their golden years and deal with a herd of alpacas. Jeff had been eager to embark on this new adventure with me, and within a short space of time, we had grown into our respective responsibilities. I dealt with the residents and their needs, and Jeff had taken on the care, and breeding, of the alpacas. We were grateful to have on staff an amazing housekeeper, Jan Young, along with a cook, and handyman.

Our apartment at the top of the renovated farmhouse was a sanctuary. I plunked myself down in my favourite chair and gazed over the fields and meadow past the barns. The sun was up, but lingering thunderclouds promised another unsettled summer day. The serenity of the view eased my anxiety that the headlines had produced.

I called back into the living room. "Come out here and join me with your coffee. Does the article provide any more details?"

He didn't need another prompt and came out with a fresh cup of coffee for me. He talked as he settled himself opposite. "The cops, as usual, are not saying much because they've just started their investigation." He drank and then put his mug down. The news had upset me but had put him in a reflective mood. "You know, I'm still disappointed that the casino was canceled there."

The potential of a casino coming to Grant's Crossing had been a bone of contention with us last year. Jeff had been all for it. I hated the idea, along with most of the lodge's residents. But I tried to remain sensitive to his disappointment. Men and their egos!

"I know, babe. But things usually work out for a reason, right? I think having a new restaurant with a spa and small resort is a great compromise. You'll still have tourists coming to town. It's not exactly a roadside diner. Anyone staying over at the resort will have money to spend. So, focus on your ideas for our Leven Lodge market stall."

He smiled and I knew the wheels were turning. Jeff and the alpacas. He loved those creatures and I had to admit he recognized a profitable business venture built around them.

I'd never let on, to him, how pleased I was there'd be no casino. In my view, it only spelled trouble for our small town. The town I'd returned to, after a long absence, and was now where I felt at home. I valued the atmosphere it had, and a casino would have cheapened, or worse quenched it.

So, Jeff could fulfill his business desires with those wooly animals, and I'd go ahead with my plans to finally put my real estate license into use. I already had the paperwork underway to set myself up with a local broker once I found one.

Our future was laid out and I was so happy thinking ahead, that I missed what he was saying.

"...tourists will love alpaca merchandise. I can do tours of our property. Endless possibilities."

I swear, the love of my life dreams about alpacas. I hoped he'd spare a dream or two about me! We were good at teasing each other, so when an opportunity presented itself...

"And will you learn how to knit alpaca blankets, and booties, for your market stall?"

Jeff offered a pretend scowl and put on his little boy's pouty face. "Very funny. I know I'm jumping the gun but..." The pout was replaced with an excited grin. "We're getting so close to the end of gestation, and the birth of the crias. I should be focusing on them. That gives us seven alpacas and we have room for a lot more!"

As I said, he dreams of alpacas. Last year he had made the acquaintance of a nearby breeder, Rick Murdock. They were thick as thieves.

"I'm sure Rick will help you when the time comes."

He drained the last of his coffee and stood. "Speaking of Rick, he plans to stop by later today. So, I'd better head to the barn."

He bent down and gave me a lingering kiss. "I do like the idea of having a high-end restaurant in town. Pubs are still my go-to, but when I want to take my best girl out for something special..."

"Your *best* girl? Ha!" I smacked his arm but smiled. "I don't want to know who the others might be."

I stood and was ready to shoo him away. I had things to take care of as well.

"I might like this kind of talk but for now, dinner plans and a massage are on hold until the investigation is over, and the place reopens. Now off you go. You may not remember, but a new resident is arriving this morning and I need to prepare. She's only here for six weeks so shouldn't be too much trouble. I'll book our massage as soon as they'll let us. Deal?"

Jeff leaned in close for a last kiss. "I'll hold you to that, babe."

***

Focus. I ran a brush through my curls and clipped them back. A light spray of cologne and I was good to go. Back to business.

A year ago, two of our rooms were left empty, and not by choice. I'd had a hit-and-miss success with finding occupants who'd fit in with the lifestyle Leven Lodge provided. Those deja vu feelings came back as I recalled the deaths brought about by a former resident, Ty Rogers. I'd nearly become one of his victims as well. He'd kidnapped me, held me at the abandoned mill, and bragged about his efforts to bring the casino to Grant's Crossing. I'd fought for my life and in the struggle, he had been killed. Ironically by the weapon he'd planned to use on me - a sedative-filled syringe.

Any wonder I was glad there'd be no casino?

Further thoughts were halted when the intercom buzzed. "Alysha? Ms. Mikado has arrived."

"I'll be right there, Jan. Thanks."

CHAPTER TWO
Dianne

July - the summer stretched ahead. More than ever, I was happy to be retired and had the freedom to enjoy lazy summer days. We'd had a doozy thunderstorm last night with teeming rain. My favourite weather. Great for sleeping, in my opinion, and good for the area farmers.

I stood in front of my bedroom window and stretched. The sun had been up a couple of hours before me. But, in the distance, thunderclouds were forming. Typical unsettled weather after a stretch of humid July heat. Alysha, and Jan, preferred the windows stay shut whenever the air conditioning was on.

Then I remembered today meant a new resident—albeit temporary—coming to Leven Lodge, where I've lived for about four years now. My curiosity over this new person was tinged with sadness, and other complicated emotions. I thought of former occupants no longer with us, especially Jock and Bea McTaggart. Jock had been a crotchety senior, but his wife was a sweetheart. They'd been gone from here for a few months now, and the place wasn't the same without them. The person arriving today would be taking over Ty Roger's old room.

Ty!

At one time a good friend, or so I had thought. Then, he betrayed all of us. Murderer! Grief counselling had been offered to us after the tragedies, but I had declined. I can take care of myself and don't need professional help to deal with life's curveballs.

Alysha, rightfully concerned about income shortage, had been a little too quick to rent the empty rooms out. Not always with a good outcome, but those *mistakes* were gone now. I hoped our expected arrival would be more to my, er, our liking.

To give her credit, she'd risen to the responsibilities as owner of the guest home which her grandmother, Estelle Grant, had established. And like Estelle, Alysha determined whoever moved in, needed to be a good fit with the existing residents. Small town living wasn't for everyone, either.

Since the first day of her arrival last year, I'd felt a connection with her—*not* motherly—more like a protective older sister. She, Jan, and I had formed a tight bond over the months.

I finished dressing, anxious to head downstairs for breakfast. Oh, and to see who was moving in, of course.

When I opened my door to the hallway, I caught a whiff - of Minnie Parker. She must have headed down just ahead of me. The whiff? Ugh. An ongoing issue that Alysha had tried to address several times, with little success. Minnie could be intimidating, and while Alysha's backbone had strengthened over the months, she still shied away from the wrath of Minnie.

Minnie's room is next to mine and we share a bathroom. In all the time I've been here, I've never seen inside her room. That's one thing, but it's the, ah, *aroma* her locked door can't contain, that gets to me. Doesn't always seem to be a concern with the other residents, but I don't think my nose is that sensitive! The smell fluctuates between unwashed body odour—which would be preferable—to stale or musty. Not unlike how an overflowing garbage can smells. And like a heavy smoker, those smells permeated her clothes. At times I envisioned the stink oozing right out of the pores in her skin. So, she was prone to leave a malodorous trail wherever she went.

I'd brought up the complaint with Alysha, and Jan, more than once, but somehow it had never been resolved. Maybe I should ask for a rent discount and see if that gets them moving. Although to be fair, the day before yesterday, Alysha assured me she had a plan and begged my patience for a few more days. Good thing I like her.

I stepped off the bottom stair and headed toward the dining room, where I was the last to arrive. Voices were excited. Like me, the rest of us wondered about our new housemate.

Leven Lodge accommodates eight residents. Currently, we were down in numbers, but the newbie arriving today would help. Philip McGee and the twins—Rose Edwards and Lily Courtemanche—sat at their places. As did Minnie.

"Sunshine all around this morning, I see." I moved to the sideboard and helped myself to coffee and a bagel. Fresh fruit sat in the middle of the spacious dining table and once I sat, I grabbed an orange.

"Dianne," acknowledged Philip, his voice monotone. He was a quiet one, often overshadowed by the energy radiating from the twins. Minnie sat taciturn, completely focused on her breakfast.

Rose had already finished eating but couldn't wait to jump right in about our new companion. "I wonder what time she'll be here. Oh, I do hope she'll be fun. This place needs to liven up." Rose and I often enjoyed time in town at the local Legion Hall. She and Lily were twins, but not identical - in looks or personality.

Minnie's butter knife clattered to her plate. "What this place needs is for a person to have some peace." And then the muttering started. "At least with the windows all shut up, there's no barn smell. Puts me off my appetite."

"And a good morning to you as well, Minnie." Oh, I was tempted to provide a comeback about smells. She was a fine one to talk. A glance around the table told me no one else was willing to broach the subject either.

Jan bustled into the dining room with trays to begin clearing away breakfast debris. If I knew her, she'd have been up extra early today to ensure the accommodation for our new housemate was all in order.

"Rushed away from my breakfast again, I see." Minnie scraped her chair back, not expecting a response, just being Minnie. We all pretty much ignored her *pleasantries* and let her be. True to form, she managed to grab another bagel before Jan cleared them away. Ewww, this time she stuck the food in her sagging sweater pocket. My own appetite took a hit and I rose from my chair as well.

"Can I give you a hand, Jan?"

"Thanks, Dianne. Everything's under control." She peeked at her watch. "You could keep an eye on the driveway and give me a shout when you see a car coming?"

"Glad to. I'll take my coffee into the front room and stand guard."

Jan laughed. "Yes, you do that."

Jan and I were closest in age, and I had grown fond of her over the years. She ran the household with precision, but still managed to ensure the home was welcoming, and a safe place for all of us. She'd been so helpful to Alysha and Jeff when they had first arrived. While she can be a private person, there's no one I'd rather have in my corner.

I settled with my coffee in the front room. The view looked out past the veranda to the long driveway. The fieldstone fireplace I sat next to is well used during colder months. In warm weather, most of us preferred the large veranda which ran the width of the house. Lots of room for everyone.

Philip entered the room, another book in hand. We had nearly lost him as well last year. A former university professor, successful despite his autism. Nice, reserved man, who doesn't always interact well with others. Ty and his bloody medicinal meddling caused Philip to have a mental crash, and he'd been hospitalized for a few months. We were glad he was back now. So was Jeff. The two of them enjoyed a strong rapport over the alpacas. Good segue.

"Are you waiting for Jeff to head out to the barn?"

"Yes. Any minute now his plane will land."

Right, I should explain that Philip has a charming range of expressions that surfaced a few years ago. Keeps us guessing at times what he means but we manage.

"Okay, but I think I saw him go there already. I guess the alpacas will be glad it's not raining?"

"To be factual, Dianne, alpacas are known to favour inclement weather."

I sat corrected and didn't respond.

With his eyes focused more on his feet than me, he left and headed for the back door, the book still in his clutches. Books, and alpacas, were his escape. Once a book's pages were opened, he was lost in whatever world he held in his hands.

I turned back to the window view and was rewarded with the sight of a large lemon heading toward the house—a brilliant yellow sports car. This might be interesting. I drained the last of my coffee and stood to get a better look as the car came to a stop at the front steps.

I called out. "Jan. Looks like she's here."

Alysha liked to use the sitting room for business when needed, so I made myself scarce, but not out of earshot.

CHAPTER THREE
Alysha

I took a deep breath and moved into view of the front door, next to Jan. I'd googled Nina Mikado, her author pseudonym for Hilary Crockett, earlier and while there were lots of photo images online, nothing prepared me for the vision standing inside my front door. I knew she had to be about fifty, even if her face tried not to show it. She was tall—but then I'm only five foot, so everyone looks tall to me—tanned, with blonde, cropped hair, sculpted into dagger-like spikes, and mascara rimmed eyes that seemed to bore right into me. I nearly forgot my manners but recovered and thrust out my hand to welcome her.

Thankfully Jan, who never lets anything faze her, stepped in. "Ms. Mikado, this is Alysha Grant, owner of Leven Lodge."

I'm glad my voice was steadier than I felt. "Ms. Mikado, lovely to meet you. No problem finding us?"

With a self-confident smile, the slim woman shook my hand. "No, no problem at all. GPS works wonders. Now then, where can I take Hemingway for a tinkle?"

My eyes were drawn to a bundle she held cocooned in her arm. I'd forgotten about the dog and had grudgingly said we'd allow it. His black beady eyes were as critical of me as the criticism I'd felt from Nina.

I didn't hesitate with a response. "As long as you avoid the flower beds and vegetable gardens, anywhere is fine. Perhaps we can set aside an area out back later?"

I'd become attuned to recognizing disapproval from Jan. Words weren't needed as she abruptly turned and headed back toward the kitchen. I felt like Moses parting the Red Sea because Nina pivoted in the opposite direction and led Hemingway down the front steps to grass barely past the flower beds.

That's when I saw her luggage parked on the veranda. It seemed extensive for a six-week stay, but maybe a lot of it had to do with her occupation. The elevator would earn its keep today.

In no time, she trod back up the steps, cooing over her companion. "There's a good doggie. Mummy is so proud of your wee-wee."

Oh, brother. I like animals, but not when they're spoiled. I made a mental note to be more selective about future residents! Then I bit my lower lip when I realized the yellow bow in its hair matched Nina's car. I could picture Dianne's eyes rolling already.

Nina scooped the dog - might be a Shih Tzu - back into her arms and when the dog coddling was done, her attention returned to me. "Ms. Grant, I apologize if I seem rude, but are you old enough to be running this place?"

Blunt *and* colourful. "Oh, I get that all the time, but rest assured I am indeed the owner of Leven Lodge. And not so formal, I'm Alysha. Follow me, and we can finalize a few formalities."

"Yes, of course. I have to say, this is a beautiful home."

"Thank you. There have been renovations over the years, but everything was done so it remained true to its original history. I'm sure you will be very comfortable."

"History? What kind of history - family secrets perhaps? Skeletons in closets? I'm always looking for new story ideas."

"No secrets here," I said as I ushered our latest guest into the room. "I meant history more in the sense of the original build of the home as a farmhouse, over one hundred years old."

"Oh, that's disappointing. But still, a house this old is bound to have stories to tell."

Ty Roger's story isn't something we openly discuss anymore. But based on Ms. Mikado's thirst for a storyline, I'd be better off dealing with it right from the start. Besides, anyone could find information about what had happened online if they wanted.

"Please, take a seat." I busied myself with my clipboard of details on Ms. Mikado. "As I said, we don't have any family secrets here, but last year we were in the news. One of our former residents turned out to be a murderer. Um, it's his former room you'll be staying in, and I hope that won't be an issue?"

Her eyes lit up. "Issue! I should say quite the opposite. I love it! I have to confess I did read up on the account and know about your close call as well." She leaned forward and patted my knee, solicitous concern etched across her face. "You poor little thing! No, wait. I have a feeling you came away the victor, am I right? Once I'm settled, I'll have lots more questions. Of course, you'll get full acknowledgment in the new book."

Hang on, I wasn't prepared for this. "New book? I know you're an author—a very successful one—but I have no intention of being the subject of a book. Please."

"Oh, relax, chickie. It will be fiction, based on fact. I'll leave your name out of it if you prefer. *The names have been changed to protect the innocent*, yada yada."

Crap and double crap. I reminded myself that I was the one in charge. So, take charge. Ignore the threat to my mental well-being for now and move on. I focused on my clipboard of information. "I believe you said your stay at Leven Lodge was for a retreat?"

"Yes, as I said, I'm working on a new book and need some peace to do so. Remove myself from the usual distractions, you know?" She petted her dog. "And Hemingway here is often my muse."

Muse. Whatever. "I hope you find Leven Lodge will fit the bill." I handed her a card with the Wi-Fi password and added, "If you have any trouble, let me know and my partner, Jeff, will have a look. He's the computer whiz around here."

She took the card. "Got it. Anything else?"

"You'll find most of the residents are more senior in age; you might not have a lot in common." And then an afterthought. "Some are not pet-friendly if you get my drift. Normally, pets aren't allowed, so an exception was made for you. Just a heads-up in case you run into any comments about...your muse."

She wiggled blood-red nails in my direction. "You'll find I'm a real people person, hon. And most people just love my little precious. He makes friends wherever we go, Anyway, age makes no difference - everyone has a story - and I love to listen."

Wow, I didn't know what kind of people person she thought she was, but she might not be an easy sell with our gang.

"Well, they love to talk. But I ask that you respect their privacy if they decline to have any input to your new book. You're here for a retreat, correct? And quiet time? All our residents value the same." I may have sounded curt, but Nina was only a temporary visitor. "I hope you understand. Now, I believe Jan has taken your luggage up to your room."

"Of course, chickie. I understand. No harm, no foul. While my previous works are cozy mysteries, I'm starting something new. I'm attracted to murder mysteries, especially around criminal and deviant behaviour. And Leven Lodge's history from last year is made to order. All to make a compelling read, but I won't bore you with the details."

Those details were *personal*, at least far as I was concerned. I'd have to keep an eye on Ms. Mikado and was already regretting my approval of her stay. Too late now. I'd have to suck it up and go with the flow. No way would I provide any information for her book. At least not intentionally.

CHAPTER FOUR
Dianne

Criminal *and* deviant behaviour? I needed to know more. And seeing as I was in the neighbourhood...

"Knock knock?" I poked my head into the room. "Sorry to interrupt, Alysha. Don't forget to remind our new guest about our cocktail hour at five?"

Alysha looked up from her paperwork. Yep, I'd intruded, based on her miffed look. Oh well. In for a penny, in for a pound.

Vibrant was the word that came to mind when I got my first good look at the woman sitting across from Alysha. She exuded an energy that would be in stark contrast with most of the residents around here. I flashed ahead to the first mealtime when we'd all be together and mentally rubbed my hands together thinking about Minnie's reaction.

Alysha introduced me to Nina Mikado. "Dianne Mitchell is our social butterfly, Nina."

Ouch. I probably deserved the dig but kept smiling. "Nice to have a new face around here, Nina. Welcome to Leven Lodge."

Her eyes sparkled. "Thank you. Did I hear you say something about a *cocktail hour*? I do like the sound of that. See you there, Dianne. We'll talk some more."

Alysha, on the other hand, was all business. "Let me show you to your room, Nina. It's one flight up, and you have a choice between stairs or the elevator."

"Excellent. Stairs will be fine. Can I say, you've been both efficient and welcoming? I believe I will be quite content during my stay. Be sure to let me know if I can fill out a survey or offer a review before I leave.

And now, I won't keep you from your day any longer. I look forward to meeting the rest of the household. And the alpacas, of course."

A tiny, menacing growl accompanied them as they breezed past me and headed toward the stairs.

I reflected on what Nina had revealed about her writing. While I enjoyed mystery and crime thrillers, cozy mysteries didn't appeal to me. But that she already knew about Ty and wanted to make us the subject of a book? Well, damn, that bothered me as much as it did Alysha.

I wandered back to the kitchen—coffee and tea were always available to us—and I needed a refill.

Or not. I arrived just in time to see Jan toss her apron on a chair. Cassie, our cook, looked as puzzled as I was. Jan was usually unflappable, and neat. To discard her apron in such a careless fashion wasn't her style. Cassie shrugged her shoulders at me. No help there. So, I followed our housekeeper as she marched to the back door and stomped outside. Her fists were clenched at her side as she stopped by a fence and leaned her arms over the rail.

I gave her a moment and then announced my presence. "Jan? Are you okay?"

Her waist-length, black braided hair shook from side to side. She seemed to be trying to compose herself. When she turned to face me, I was stunned to see her eyes red-rimmed and her face puffy. Jan crying?

I moved closer to her. "What's wrong?"

"Not the best of mornings, Dianne."

"Tell me. Maybe I can help."

She put her head back as if she could find the answer in the overcast sky above. "Where to start."

I felt raindrops, the clouds overhead threatened to open. "How about we go back inside and find a quiet corner?"

She nodded and moved past me. "Come." I followed her back into the house and we moved into the main floor living quarters she shares with Cassie.

"Have a seat."

I obliged and waited.

She was still upset. "I'll have to apologize to Cassie. I snapped at her over something, not her fault, but that dog was the last straw!"

Ah, now we were getting somewhere. "I'm surprised Alysha allowed it. Not that I mind, but not so sure about the others if you know what I mean."

Upset and now disapproving. "You should know by now, I will support Alysha's decision about the residents here, Dianne." Oops, once again I'd been put in my place.

"Well, after all, it's only a temporary stay, right? But there must be something else bothering you."

Her face grew tight. "It's about the body found."

"Why - did you know him?" Maybe a stupid question, but I had to ask.

"I know they haven't released the victim's name, but I know of his family. From back home."

"The reserve, you mean?"

She nodded. From what I knew of Jan, she was protective of her family. Proud of her heritage, and not afraid to stand up to anyone - or anything - who threatened it. She'd been more relieved than Alysha when the casino was scratched. It would have been an irresistible draw for many, and she had real concerns.

"His name is - was - Andrew Makwa. His grandparents are close friends with my parents."

"I'm sorry, Jan. Truly."

She uttered a small laugh. "Just when I felt relieved about no casino. But if I'm to be honest, it's not just the casino. The problems run deeper. Andrew had minor run-ins with the law over illegal drug use. More with the crowd he associated with, in my opinion. And now another young life is gone. I hope I'm proved wrong, but I fear there will be a connection.

I didn't reply, unsure of what I could say. She looked at me as if reading my thoughts. "I know, not your problem, is it?"

"I wouldn't say that. Drugs are a problem with young people everywhere, but I realize there are extra pressures with many." I told myself to shut up before I put my foot in it. The safest bet would be to let her vent. And not for the first time did I wonder whether it was a good thing I'd never been a parent.

She took a breath and when she continued her voice had a resigned quality. "Mostly the younger ones who can't see their future. They grow discouraged and are easy prey for the escape that drugs provide." She clenched her jaw. "If I could, I would round up all the drug dealers and..and... Oh, I don't know what I would do with them, that wouldn't land me in jail!"

"You - in jail? Nope. Can't happen. Who would clean around here?"

The worry lines on Jan's face faded and she smiled at me. "I'm sorry, didn't mean to dump this on you. But you did ask."

I breathed a little easier, the tension had eased.

"I did. I might not have any advice, but I always have a shoulder."

She stood. "Thank you for that. Now, the day is waiting. I need to get into town and the drive will help clear my head. Oh, and by the way, Alysha's found a way to get into Minnie's room."

She didn't elaborate, but *my* day had certainly improved!

CHAPTER FIVE
Alysha

After Nina inspected her room, she more or less hustled me out. "The room's perfect, but if you don't mind, I'm wiped after my drive. A short rest before dinner is in order. Five o'clock for cocktails, you said? See you then."

I was glad to escape with no idea why I felt relieved to be away from her. Her personality was intense, and it wasn't a stretch to see how different Nina was from the others who lived here. Although, I thought she and Dianne might share some qualities. I wondered what dinner time would be like with our newest resident, but my main concern was finding out what had Jan in a bother. So, I dropped by the kitchen to see if I could have a word with her, but I was too late. Cassie informed me she'd left for town to pick up a parcel from the post office.

Pouring me a cup of coffee, Cassie continued chattering. "I'd stay clear of her if I was you. She's in a strange mood - nearly bit my head off about using too much dish soap. No idea what she's *really* upset about."

"You're right, that doesn't sound like her. When she gets back, can you ask her to come and see me? I'll be upstairs for a while doing paperwork."

"Sure, I'll let her know."

My intent to escape was delayed when Cassie's curiosity kicked in. "Hey. Our newest guest. What's she like? I saw her fancy sports car. Crazy bright yellow! And she has a dog. And what about the body? Wonder who it is, or if I know him?"

Cassie tends to gossip. Something I don't condone. "Stop right there. Ms. Mikado has a dog—Hemingway—and drives a sports car. Period. As for the body, let's leave it to the police, okay? I'd prefer you remember to set another place at the table. A special *welcome* meal would be nice for our newest resident."

Reprimands rolled off her like water off a duck. "Do you have any suggestions, because I had thought about a veggie casserole with pasta?"

Cassie had a reputation for unorthodox creations. Sometimes we're not sure what we're eating. "She hasn't indicated any preferences, so I'll leave it with you. Now, is there anything else I can help you with?"

"No no, I'm fine. Oh, better let her know about the cocktail hour. Then the crew can meet her before dinner."

I smiled at Cassie. "You're not just a pretty face. Thanks for the reminder but Dianne's already invited her."

Cassie had a mischievous look on her face and mumbled as she turned away, "Wish I'd been a fly on the wall when Dianne invited her, bet she'll have something to say.

I give up - Cassie will never stop wanting to gossip. I sighed, took my coffee, and headed upstairs.

***

I tried to settle at Uncle Dalton's old desk but was not in the mood for accounting. I couldn't concentrate. Current income from the home left little profit margin, so adding new residents had to be a top priority. Especially if Jeff's plans to expand the herd with more breeding of the alpacas are to be realized. Rooms standing empty weren't helping. Recent experience with taking in guests had taught me a few lessons. I needed to be more diligent. And no pets!

I read over a few applications on our new website, but my mind kept traveling back to the sawmill and events of last year. *Another body!*

After spinning my wheels and getting nowhere, I needed a break, so I changed into my running gear. I thought Jeff might go for a run with me. A good way to burn off steam and clear mental cobwebs. He'd still be with the alpacas, so I headed in the direction of his favourite hang-out.

As I drew nearer to the barn, I stopped for a minute to admire the changes Jeff had wrought over the past year. Fresh paint, some boards replaced, and a general tidy-up had done wonders to make the place almost inviting. It might be the alpacas' home, but I sensed it had become an oversized man-cave.

A man-cave with added features most men wouldn't boast about. Because there was my man mucking out the byre and smiling! Our three males and two heavily pregnant female alpacas were happy wandering in the pasture. All of the wooly heads popped up to see me, but curiosity satisfied, they went back to the task at hand, or hoof.

"Hey, you." He looked up when I spoke. "I wondered if you had time to run with me?"

He leaned on the pitchfork. "Sorry, you're on your own with the run today. I'm expecting Rick any minute to check the girls."

Rick Murdock, and his wife Amelia, operated an alpaca breeding farm nearby and had helped Jeff with all things alpaca related. As a side benefit, the four of us had formed a good friendship.

I nodded. "Right. You'll be happy to have him on hand for any unexpected complications at the births."

His eyes lit up. "Exciting, isn't it? Not long now until they arrive. Mags and Junebug seem fine, but Rick will give them the once over. He's seen lots of births. Me not so much."

I laughed. "You'll have to think of names for their offspring. Okay, I'm off. I'll be back in an hour."

"We'll have a run together soon. I promise. Oh, before you go. I assume our new arrival is here?"

"She has checked in and I'll have to fill you in later, sorry." I pecked him on the cheek. "I'd best be off. I don't want to get caught in a thunderstorm."

Good timing. Just then, Rick Murdock's truck rumbled past me on his way to see Jeff. We shared a wave.

I soon broke out in a sweat pounding the pavement on my way into town. A few early afternoon shoppers made their way to cars parked at the curb. I hesitated when I saw a newspaper stand outside the convenience store declaring *Body Found On Grounds of New Spa.*

Normally I enjoyed the solitude a run provided, but not today. My mind jumped all over the place with so much to think about. Not the least, was my long-held goal of establishing myself as a real estate broker. I had the license, just needed to refresh on a few things. Grant's Crossing wouldn't know what hit them.

I paused to drink from my water bottle but kept my legs pumping.

The sky had grown ominous. Several fat drops of rain landed on me, and the wind had picked up. Looked like we were in for the predicted rain and more thundery weather. I decided to cut my run short. Heading back to the farmhouse, I anticipated a shower and a change of clothes. By now, Jan should be back, and I could ask what had upset her. I sensed it had to be more than Nina and her dog. Maybe she'd learned of Nina's plan to fictionalize our awful experiences of last year. That would be more than enough to upset her.

Never a dull moment at Leven Lodge.

***

I was barely out of the shower when Jeff returned to our quarters and began badgering me for details about Nina.

I threw my hands up in mock surrender. "Chill. All I'm going to tell you is that she is an author, and she has brought her muse with her." Okay, so a small part of me liked to tease and it was fun to see the exasperated look on his face.

"A muse?"

"Yep. Her muse has a name. Hemingway. Big-name for a tiny, spoiled, and pampered dog. But you can form your own opinion. Here's a suggestion. Why don't you bring a few beers to our pre-dinner cocktail hour? You may have found a soul mate. But be warned. She might ask you questions about last year. She's writing a book about it. This is your time to be famous. *Hero, Jeff Iverson, rescues his love!*"

"You're not serious, are you? I'm thinking there's no way you'd want to be the focus of anything written about last year?"

He was right. I shouldn't even joke about it. He knew me better than anyone and I agreed I wanted no part of any book.

"That's what I thought, babe, so I'll pass on the notoriety, thanks. However, the beer is a good idea since the bar cart only supplies spirits. Ugh. No idea how anyone drinks that stuff. Give me a good lager any day."

Now that we had Nina out of the way, I turned the tables on him. "Your turn. Did you have a productive visit with Rick?"

Jeff grinned from ear to ear and made a move to start tickling me. He knows I hate it and only made the pretense of an attack. "Maybe I won't say."

I knew I was in for teasing—his boyish grin was a dead giveaway.

"Seeing as you're keeping things from me, I should do the same." He grew serious. "Back to the writer. What kind of dog did she bring? Sorry, babe, but I can't have a dog near the alpacas. According to Rick, alpacas and cats are great together, but dogs—not so much."

"It's only a small dog, maybe a Shih Tzu? I'll make sure Nina's been told to keep the pooch away from them. Okay?"

"They'll appreciate it, thanks."

"And by *they*, you mean your wooly charges?" I knew the answer, but the bantering hadn't quite finished.

He moved in for a cuddle, but I pushed him away. "We'll get back to this later, but right now, I want a word with Jan before dinner, and it's almost five. I'm surprised she never came up here, I did ask Cassie to tell her. And a suggestion? You might want to hit the shower or risk smelling like *eau de Minnie*."

My suggestion was met with a teasing slap to my rear as I walked away.

****

Downstairs, Cassie said Jan waited for me in their sitting room. I tapped on the door leading to their rooms.

Jan's quiet voice beckoned me in. She sat in her favourite chair, and at first, her face was void of emotion. But then her eyes caught mine and her beautiful smile returned.

She started to laugh. "Alysha, little one, don't look so worried."

"Are you alright? I *was* worried, especially when you pretty much disappeared all day. Did I do something to upset you?"

"You weren't the cause of my irritability earlier. Although I admit I have no fondness for the dog Nina Mikado has in tow. I know you have the final say on our guests and I will support you, but—be warned. If that excuse for a dog soils my gardens, she will hear about it!"

"I'm on the same page regarding the dog, Jan, and I told her as much. Um, perhaps I should mention Nina wants to write her newest book about events from last year. She knows I won't participate. But she'll be digging."

Her face darkened. "And she'll get nothing from me. You didn't know this ahead of time?"

"Believe me, if I'd known that was her intent, she'd not be here. I am sorry."

She stood, smoothed her apron, and extended a hand. I reached for it. Her voice was tinged with sadness. "I breathed easier when the casino development was revised, you know."

How could I forget the unrest the potential casino had caused among so many? Including Jeff and me. She and I had both been pleased when the town council approved the development changes from a casino to an upscale spa, including a restaurant and small overnight resort. Our reasons may have been different, but I think it helped strengthen a bond between us.

"I know you were. So, what else is bothering you? I feel there's a connection."

She patted my hand and released it. "Ironic. No casino, but still trouble in the area. I'm surprised Dianne hasn't already told you. I talked to her about it earlier today. You see, I know the family of the young man found dead on the grounds."

Her reason for being upset made sense. Jan has a fierce loyalty to her family, close and extended.

"No, I haven't seen much of Dianne today. Do you know the family well?"

"My parents do. I've talked with them, and they tell me his family is taking this very hard. Familiar story. They'd wanted Andrew to continue with school, but he was more interested in finding a job. Apparently, there were also drug issues - at least among some of Andrew's circle. And that's where I feel there is a connection, as you say."

"If you need to take some time to be with your family, it's okay."

Her face relaxed and she smiled. "Thank you, for now, I'll stay here. I'll let you know if that changes?"

"Of course, Jan. Anything I can do to help, let me know."

I struggled with wanting to provide comfort and also knowing household demands never stopped. It was time to focus on the home front. A distraction might help Jan more than I could.

"I will admit I'm relieved you'll be on hand during dinner this evening. Adding Nina, I foresee friction. They'll all have seen the paper, too, so we may have our hands full."

Jan's humour was back. "Agreed. I'd better keep the antacids and headache remedies at hand."

CHAPTER SIX
Dianne

I'd come to enjoy our pre-dinner cocktail hour. Usually reserved for Friday evenings, we might also gather throughout the week for a special occasion. Especially in the summertime when a cool drink was most welcome. If it hadn't been pouring rain, we'd have been on the veranda.

Tonight, though, we were meeting in one of the two front rooms. One I like to call the media room because it holds a large screen TV and super sound system. Comfy recliners are the order of the day there! The choice this evening is for the cozier room, with a fireplace. And it's better suited for socializing.

Tantalizing aromas wafted down the hall from the kitchen as I moved over to the bar cart and checked out available selections. Lots of ice in the bucket as well. Jan, or Alysha, had done well stocking the cart. Why would I live anywhere else?

It was almost five o'clock, and the others would be here any minute. I fixed a martini, and planted myself in my favourite wingback chair, next to the room's beautiful fireplace. And waited. Who would arrive first? It might be fun if Ms. Mikado showed up last and I could relish all the reactions.

I heard Rose and Lily before they arrived. Rose's voice overshadowed her sister's. Yakking about an upcoming episode of Jeopardy.

"Drinks, ladies?"

"That martini looks fine, Dianne. I'll have the same. Lily—you'll have your usual soda?"

Lily merely nodded. Sometimes I wondered if underneath her mostly meek exterior, she'd rather be more like her sister. Or was she content always being in her shadow? I bet they had an interesting childhood. Maybe I'd steer the author in their direction and away from the murders.

I fixed the martini and passed a ginger ale to Lily. In quick succession, Philip and Minnie arrived. Never understood why Minnie bothered joining us. She doesn't get along with anyone. Her hobby seems to be annoying people so maybe that's it.

"Dianne, have you seen our new housemate yet?" Rose's curiosity was in overdrive. I noticed she'd applied a heavier coat than normal of her fire-engine red lipstick. Cassie will complain again about the dishwasher not cleaning it all off the glasses!

Before I could reply, Nina Mikado breezed into the room. Rose's jaw dropped and Lily's eyes popped wider than I'd ever seen. Philip glanced up, blinked once, and put his nose back into his book.

"Here I am. Nina Mikado, in the flesh."

Boy, that's self-confidence - to assume her reputation preceded her. She's in for a tough crowd. Once they got past her raccoon eyes and flowered yoga pants, that is. The flowing yellow scarf was an extra touch. Maybe I should have a signature colour, too.

I decided to live up to my designated *social butterfly* status. "Nina, glad you can join us. I'll do the introductions and then fix you a drink. What'll you have?"

She eyed the cart while acknowledging the others as I went around the room.

"Not seeing anything you like?" I asked when she didn't voice a preference.

"Maybe she'd like a pole to dance with," sneered Minnie.

Nina's head snapped round to see where that came from. "Takes one to know one?"

Holy cow! Minnie's mouth gaped like a fish out of water. Get the matches, the fireworks were set to go.

Not missing a beat, Nina turned back to the bar cart. "No tequila I see. Not that I expected a fully stocked bar, but tequila's my go-to preference. It's what *works* for me, know what I mean? Maybe a beer then?"

"Did someone say beer?" Jeff and Alysha had joined us. Jeff swung a small bucket with a few beer bottles, in one hand, and held Alysha's hand with the other.

"Ah, a man after my own heart. Perfect." She grabbed one of the icy cold bottles.

I watched Jeff and Alysha exchange glances and wondered what Alysha had told him about Nina.

Alysha introduced Jeff and while they got acquainted, I stole a look at Minnie. She'd not said another word but sat with her ever-present knitting bag and kept her eyes glued on Nina. Ignorance must be bliss because Nina would have no way of knowing the wizened old creature in the corner was likely plotting a comeback of epic proportions.

"All settled in now, Nina?" asked Alysha.

"Thanks, chickie. We love the room. This place will be perfect for writing, and I can't wait to get started on my new book."

"Book?" Philip looked up. "You write?"

"That I do, cowboy. Mostly cozies." She glanced at the book in his lap. "What are you into?"

He never quite made eye contact with her. "Animals. Any and all."

"Philip taught animal husbandry, university level." Alysha jumped in to explain. I bet she wanted to head off a Philip-ism.

"Good for you," said Nina. Before she could ask more, a question came her way from Lily.

"Nina? You said *we* love the room. I thought, that is, we were told... Well, aren't you here by yourself?"

Sometimes the quiet ones pick up what others miss. I'm glad it was Lily asking her and not Minnie, who continued to knit at an accelerated pace and had narrowed eyes only for Nina.

"It's Lily, right? Yes, I did say *we*. So, here, meet Hemingway."

No one had noticed, when she trounced into the room, she cradled the toy-sized dog underneath her scarf. Philip started at the news but reached out a hand to pet the snow-white hair of the dog. Anyone who knew Philip wouldn't have been surprised at the gentle look on his face. The same relaxed face he shows around the alpacas. For him, animals were much easier to connect with than humans.

Lily stepped forward. "Oh, what a sweetheart. Can I pet him?"

Nina nodded and Lily let Hemingway sniff her hand before she patted the top of his head. I can't remember the last time I'd seen her smile. Tremors of delight coursed through the dog's tiny frame as he lapped up Lily's attention.

But the reprieve from Minnie was too good to last. She slapped her knitting on her lap and began to push it all into the worn bag she carries around with her. "I pay good money for peace around here. Yappy dogs don't belong." True to form, Minnie called a spade a spade. At the sound of her voice, Hemingway reacted in kind.

"Hush now baby, be nice. We all have to get along for the next few weeks," Nina cooed. Better that Nina focuses on her dog than add fuel to Minnie's fire.

"Well, I don't have to get along with it." Minnie grabbed her knitting bag. "It better not be in the dining room while we eat." She scurried from the room in a huff.

Alysha interceded. "I'm sorry, Nina. You'll have to excuse Minnie. She speaks her mind, and while we are used to it, it can be unsettling. But I will have to insist that Hemingway not be in the dining room—he's welcome anywhere else."

Nina's eyes glittered. "I kind of like her. She'd be a great character in my book. Hmmm—victim, or murderer?" Then she fussed at the dog again. "Sorry, baby. You'll have to stay in our room for a little while, but mummy will be back as soon as I can."

She gulped the rest of her beer. "I'll meet you all in the dining room—sans Hemingway."

And that was our introduction to Nina Mikado. Dinner might be fun, or a total disaster.

***

In the dining room, it was nice to have another chair occupied at the table. Only two empty chairs this evening. Nina sat across from Minnie. I kept glancing between the two of them. Minnie glared at her between mouthfuls of food. Nina was nonplussed by the attention. Minnie had a short fuse, but Nina? The evening was all about her. *I've done this, I've been here, I've met so and so.* Not much room to ask her any questions. Look up self-absorbed in the dictionary—that's her. She had to stop for air at some point. I was ready.

I laid my fork down and pounced. "So, Nina. A new book? What are you writing about?" Alysha would be annoyed at me for stirring the pot, but if the fancy-pants writer was going to be with us for a while, I for one, wanted to know where we stood with her, with no hidden agenda.

Our dinner of baked macaroni and cheese, with bacon and salads, was forgotten. A perfect intermission before dessert.

Nina clapped her hands together. "Thanks for asking, Dianne. Love your highlights by the way. Do you have a salon in the village, or do you go elsewhere? I might need a referral." She raked her fingers through the blonde tips of her own coiffure. "Six weeks, roots. You know." She winked at me.

Say what now? *Village*? I didn't care about her stupid roots. I wanted the dirt on her new book.

"Your book?"

"Yes, of course. Sorry." She glanced around the table. "I have to confess it's no accident I'm here. I've read up on what happened last year, and I want to base a new murder mystery on all of you! Isn't that great?"

For some reason, all eyes turned to Minnie. Her jaw had stopped chewing, and her eyes were like slits. "You have no right. Folks need their privacy respected. Mark my words, missy, you'll regret this. Lost my appetite, thanks to you." Her gnarled index finger pointed at Nina. "I'm done here, prefer my own company. And keep that dog out of my way, or else."

Alysha tried to smooth things over. "Minnie, please stay. Dessert is coming. Your favourite, rice pudding."

"Not hungry." She turned and left the dining room. She was beyond upset. Normally, she'll grab some food items off the sideboard, but she bypassed a selection of cookies as if they were invisible.

At that moment Jan came into the room with a large serving bowl. I didn't miss the bemused look she gave Alysha, but her voice was pure Jan. "Anyone for a bowl of warm rice pudding?"

And Nina? As if not a harsh word had been said. Although the heightened colour of her cheeks said otherwise. "So, other than Minnie, who wants to be in my book?"

CHAPTER SEVEN
Alysha

Over the past several months, it had become routine for Jan, Dianne, and me to spend an hour or two together at day's end to catch up, reflect, or speculate on events at Leven Lodge. Not every day, mind you, but at least a couple of times a week. Often in Jan's living quarters or one of the two front rooms. In nicer weather, we'd sometimes take our discussion along for an evening walk. I'd come to enjoy these times and usually looked forward to them.

There was no question that this evening we had to talk. I knew there'd be loads to discuss, and while tempting, I'd have to refrain from it turning into a gossip session.

Cassie had gone into town to help out at the Crossings Tavern, which her father owns, so Jan's room would be private. Jeff had nightly alpaca duties, and my time was my own.

I needed to vent! "I'll take some of those antacids if you have them handy, Jan. I could kick myself for allowing that woman access to our home! How *dare* she even think of using us to exploit our painful experiences. I hate to ever agree with Minnie, but she's right. We are entitled to our privacy, and Nina Mikado wants to take advantage of us for her own gain."

Jan gave me a welcomed, motherly hug. "Calm down, little one. I think among the three of us we can manage one skinny blonde. And I volunteer to keep an eye on her *baby*."

A mental image of Jan chasing after Hemingway made me smile, and I relaxed.

"I assume she had references?" asked Dianne.

"She did. Three, and all glowing. I suppose they'd have no way of knowing she had ulterior motives though."

"Are they ulterior? I mean she's been upfront about it since she arrived. Different story if we didn't find out until she'd been here a while. After all, she could have asked perfectly innocent questions, and if no one knew she was doing research, we'd have been none the wiser, right?" Dianne was right. Nina hadn't tried to hide anything. But still. I was annoyed at myself.

Jan's wisdom trumped my regret. "This is all part of the learning experience. If it makes you feel any better, I bet Estelle would not have done anything differently. So don't berate yourself. Just move on."

"Do you think so, Jan? You're not just saying it to make me feel better?"

"I will never steer you wrong, little one. I see traits of Dalton and Estelle in you more and more. I know you are meant to be here, and I am meant to support you as long as I can."

My throat tightened and I didn't trust myself to speak, so I nodded. I was filled with gratitude for Jan. Dianne hadn't chimed in with any opinion, but I was also grateful for her friendship.

The lodge had settled for the night. Jeff would be putting the alpacas to bed, the twins were probably engrossed in their game shows, and who knows where Philip had gone to read his book. And Minnie? Likely sulking in her room. As for Nina, I assumed there would be a bathroom break for Hemingway to interrupt her writing. I hoped I wouldn't run into her before tomorrow.

Time to get back on track. I turned to Dianne. "So, you're not sticking up for Nina, are you?" I smiled to let her know I was kidding, or was I?

She laughed. "Kiddo, I don't know her nearly well enough to say one way or the other. You and Jan are in charge, so lead on."

I complied with Dianne's directive. "Okay then, ladies, out with it. I don't approve of gossip, but I'd like your opinions regarding our writer in residence."

We'd gone through a great deal in the past year, and I'd learned to rely on their take on situations and people. In my mind, we were a good team. Jan had moved to a side table, returning with a small liqueur bottle, and three tiny glasses. She wasn't much of a drinker, so I was a little surprised to watch her dispense the amber liquid. A faint hint of orange tickled my nose. Replacing the bottle's cork, she handed one to me. "This might help more than an antacid."

Dianne had perked up when she took her glass from Jan. "Are we celebrating something?"

A gentle smile spread over Jan's face as she lifted her glass. "No, not celebrating. But you both looked like you needed something, and I only share this bottle with special friends. Cheers."

Dianne and I lifted our glasses and sipped the precious offering. "Cheers," we said in unison.

Jan settled in her recliner. "Now before we say more on our dog lady, I have a few other items on my agenda."

"Agenda?" Dianne glanced at the bottle. "I'll need more if we have an *agenda.*"

Dianne and I looked at each other, and then she said what I was thinking. "It's not like you to play guessing games Jan. Tell us then, what's the first thing on your agenda."

"I had intended my news to be fun, but the discovery of Andrew's body on the restaurant grounds has taken the wind out of my sails."

Dianne and I didn't interrupt but let her continue.

"And now I'm not sure I want to go ahead with my plan. Perhaps it wasn't meant to be. You'll say it's out of character for me anyway." She sipped her drink.

Dianne leaned forward. "You and I have been around long enough to know that life always goes on. It doesn't stop for tragedy or loss. And maybe whatever you had planned should still take place. Tell us?"

Indecision showed in her eyes and the set of her mouth. "Promise you won't laugh?"

I crossed my heart. "I promise, and you do as well, right, Dianne?"

"Absolutely."

A small smile twitched at the corner of Jan's mouth. "Right. I'm giving you two notice that at the first opportunity, I'm treating myself to a spa day. A massage and a pedi or mani, or whatever they call it. Maybe even a facial."

Dianne laughed, and I think she sounded relieved that it was only a spa day Jan wanted. I don't know about her, but I had visions of something way more dramatic. Like an elopement or something, she'd kept hidden.

"Oh, Jan. That's terrific." Dianne's eyes brightened. "Perhaps the three amigos can all have a spa day together. It's no secret I enjoy pampering, and I've no complaints about Amy's services at *Heaven Sent*, in town. But a full day at a spa? Yep, I could get into that."

"You'd both go with me? I'd like that."

Seeing her shoulders drop made me realize she'd been tense about the whole subject. I'm not a spa person, but the thought of a day away from the cares of Leven Lodge might be good for all of us.

Then reality returned, and the smile disappeared from Jan's face. She reached for the liqueur bottle again. "Of course, until the investigation is complete, there'll be no bookings. I'll likely be attending a funeral in the meantime."

That quickly dampened my spirits as well. "First things first. Any inside information from your nephew, Jan?" Dakotah Young - Dax - was a Detective Constable with the local police.

"I've texted him, but of course, there is very little he can say right now. He has promised to keep me informed when there is news to share."

I declined the offer of another drink, but Dianne had no qualms about a refill.

Jan finished her drink and put her glass down. "For now, though, the spa day is on hold."

Dianne responded. "I smell a *but* coming. We're all ears Jan. What's next?"

"Where to start. Alysha, you know I will always back you with your choice of guests but this one - she sure is different. I'm not thrilled with having a dog here but will handle it because it's only for six weeks. This is a place of retirement where the residents like some quiet time. Her lifestyle isn't conducive."

"Jan, you know I had no idea of her plan when I agreed to rent her the room. But she's here now, so we'll need to suck it up. Remember, she is a writer—and I'd rather have a good review of Leven Lodge than a negative one. We don't know her reach or influence. Dianne?"

"I agree. She won't get any information from me for her book, but I have to say, I like how she changes the dynamics around here. Conversation at mealtime can be dull with my usual companions. It should be an interesting few weeks. Perhaps we should get some tequila in for Ms. Mikado. Or is it Hilary Crockett? That's her real name. I looked her up." Dianne tilted her glass back and finished her drink. "Next time I'm in town, I'll grab a bottle of tequila."

I chuckled. "Let's move on to the next item on Jan's agenda. This should cheer you up, Dianne."

"You're going to introduce me to a dashing millionaire, and we'll sail off into the sunset together?"

I smiled at them both and told Dianne I couldn't quite arrange for the millionaire. "Would getting into Minnie's room tomorrow make up for your disappointment?"

"Hell, yes! Music to my ears. How did you manage to get her permission?"

"All will be revealed tomorrow."

Jan looked relieved and started clearing away the glasses. "If you don't mind ladies, I'm going to watch the news before bed. We've covered all the items, so tomorrow we'll see what unfolds."

Dianne and I said goodnight and headed to our rooms. As my grandmother would say, tomorrow is another day.

CHAPTER EIGHT
Dianne

I couldn't ignore the relentless, high-pitched, barking any longer and threw my covers to one side. Sleep was a distant memory, and I longed for more. At first, I thought the barking came from across the hall, but then it registered as coming from outside.

I padded over and opened the window a bit to enjoy the fresh scent lingering after the rain. Couldn't see anything, but my ears worked. In between the yips and snarls—large sounding for such a small dog—I made out Nina's voice urging Hemingway to shut up. The nurturing and coddling tone I'd heard previously was strangely absent now.

I closed the window. For a moment, I debated crawling back beneath the still warm covers. Until I remembered that today Alysha was going to breach Minnie's room. I couldn't wait and was glad of motivation to get myself dressed and ready for the day.

Breakfast wouldn't be for a couple of hours yet, but if the coffee wasn't on the go by the time I headed downstairs, I'd get it started myself. Wouldn't be the first time.

Dinner last night had been more entertaining than anything I'd seen on TV, or online, in quite a while. Minnie may have met her match with Nina Mikado. Who knew what would play out over the next few weeks?

I made my way quietly down the stairs. Couldn't smell any coffee, but someone was rustling around in the kitchen. I headed there expecting to see either Jan or Cassie. Instead, I saw a ghost.

At least, the white face mask Nina wore made me think so. She held a squirming Hemingway in her grasp under the kitchen sink faucet. Shit—she'd better not let Jan see that. Because shit was the word. The dog was covered. Filthy, more grey than white. She hadn't seen me yet and cooed over the lump of wet fur.

"What a naughty boy you are. You know there's no digging allowed. And see? Your nails are a dreadful mess. Tsk, tsk. I don't think we'll find a *PawsSpa* in this neck of the woods. Now, give me that."

I watched as she yanked a tattered piece of cloth from the mighty jaws. The mighty, dirty jaws. Then she spotted me and startled, let the cloth fall to the floor.

"Dianne. Sorry, did I wake you?"

Should I, shouldn't I? "No, I'm just in search of coffee. If you're through with the sink, I'll put the first pot on. And a word to the wise. Jan is fastidious over her kitchen—you'd best not leave a trace of bath time. Maybe you didn't notice the mudroom by the back door? Next time, I'd use that."

"Yes. Of course. No. My bad, then. I didn't notice the mudroom when I came in."

Of course, I couldn't help it and glanced at her feet. Yep. Almost as muddy as the mutt. And then I saw the tracks from the back door. If Jan wasn't impressed with her arrival yesterday, this wouldn't help. Not that I wanted to help Nina, but Jan didn't need to start her day on the wrong foot, or feet.

"Listen, Jan will be here any minute. Finish cleaning up the sink, and I mean spotless. I'll grab a mop for the floor."

She had the grace to look guilty, although it was hard to tell under the dried and cracking paste on her face. Hemingway was now clean and subdued. Nestled into some kind of sling thing Nina wore around her neck.

A few minutes later we were done. Nina and the pooch had left, the floor was clean, and I started making coffee. Just as Jan arrived, tying up her apron.

"Good morning, Dianne. You're up early?"

I said a silent prayer that she'd find nothing amiss, then turned to greet her. "One of those days when I couldn't sleep in. Is it bad to admit I'm excited about Alysha's exploration of Minnie's room?"

Jan smiled but didn't comment.

Breakfasts were a busy time, so I grabbed my coffee and left her to it. "I'll get out of your hair. Unless you need any help?"

"Go enjoy your coffee. And the solitude. Cassie will be along shortly."

***

"These scrambled eggs are delicious. I think I'll have some more." Nina stood and moved to the sideboard.

Minnie pursed her lips and I waited in anticipation of a comment. But nothing. She went back to attacking her plate of food. In fact, I realized now she'd been unusually quiet ever since she sat down.

We had a full table, including Jeff and Alysha.

I couldn't resist. "Busy day ahead, Alysha?"

She ignored the dig. "Oh, the usual. Always lots to do around here. Nothing to concern yourself with." But the slight upturn to her lips told me she was wise to my devilish prod.

Normal breakfast chit-chat followed. Talk about the weather, and of course, speculation about the body found earlier in the week.

Rose pushed aside her empty plate. "What a shame about that young man. So sad for his family, too. Whoever they are."

No way would I let on Jan had the information Rose was fishing for.

"We never had this kind of problem when we were that age, did we, Rose?"

Rose laughed at her sister's question. "As if we'd even be allowed to hear about news like that. From *our* parents?"

"I suppose you're right, as usual."

Rose explained for the benefit of the rest of the table. "Our parents had the misguided notion their daughters should be protected from anything unpleasant. They were ahead of their time and even had us home-schooled so we would never be bullied or suffer a schoolyard scrape. Lily here always defends them, but I say they did more harm than good, raising us that way."

"They did what they thought best," said Lily. The resigned quality to her voice had probably been ingrained for years. Like I've said, I bet those two had an interesting childhood.

Rose changed the subject. "Anyway, I hope the investigation wraps up soon so the spa can reopen. I'm anxious to try out some of the services they offer."

"Maybe they can do something about those wrinkles," sniped Minnie.

"At least I know what a spa is for," retorted Rose.

I settled back to watch the show, but Nina broke things up. "Now ladies. Let's not bicker. Life's too short. I'd hoped to make use of the spa while I'm here as well, but if it doesn't work out, c'est la vie. That's French you know." The barb hit its mark with Minnie.

"Well kiss my derriere. That's French too." Minnie smirked. Then she exited the room. I noticed Lily's small grin as she watched our wicked witch's departure.

I had a feeling breakfast congeniality was done.

***

After the breakfast crowd dispersed, I sought out Alysha. She'd returned to her apartment at the top of the house. I knocked on her door. "Alysha? It's just me. Can I come in?"

She smiled when she saw me. "I bet you're here about Minnie. Want to tag along when I have it out with her about her room?"

She had to ask? "If you'll let me. I've been waiting for this a long time."

"I know. And so have the others. I must admit, she still can intimidate me. But she won't be able to refuse me this time."

She moved over to her desk and picked up an official document, issued by Grant's Crossing Fire Department, and let me read it.

Mandatory smoke detector installation in the residents' rooms. Not just for Minnie, but all of us.

I smiled and clapped my hands. "When do we start?"

"I'm waiting on Jan, and Frank, who has agreed to do the installations. This means your room as well."

Frank Adams was our gardener and minor handyman. He'd long known Alysha's family and was getting on in years. Despite arthritis and a slower pace, he also seemed to enjoy lending a hand with the alpacas. I didn't know much more about him. He was a kind soul, and always willing to lend a hand.

"I think four of us should be enough of an army to squash any resistance from Minnie. Well-played, Alysha!"

***

Thirty minutes later, our army stood outside the offensive door. Jan held the smoke detector, Frank had the step ladder, and Alysha gripped the fire department directive. Me, I just held back.

Jan knocked. "Minnie. It's Jan. Please open the door."

The 'no' was muffled, but adamant. "I'm busy."

Alysha stepped forward. Frank shot me a grin as if to say, *here we go*.

"Minnie, it's Alysha. I must insist you open the door. You were told yesterday about the smoke detector. A building code requirement. If we are to keep Leven Lodge operational, these are to be installed. Today."

"No need for that thing in my room. I'm entitled to my privacy."

Jan sighed. "Not at the expense of others' safety. Minnie, I have the key and am coming in. This has gone on long enough. If we don't come in today, then I'm afraid you'll need to find other living accommodation."

Silence from the other side. Then a scraping sound. Had she forced a chair against the door? I think we were all holding our breath.

The lock clicked, and the door opened a crack. No wonder we held our breath! If a smell could be visible...this would be it. Her wrinkled face poked out. "Brought the whole town, did you? Maybe I should look for another home where I wouldn't be bothered all hours."

"That's your privilege Minnie, but for today, and right now, we need to install this." Jan held the smoke detector under Minnie's nose. "Let us in, please."

I couldn't see much over Minnie's shoulder; her room was in darkness. The door opened a little more, and then Jan pushed forward. Quickly followed by Alysha and Frank. I was tempted as well but knew I didn't have any reason. At least with the door open, I could see, sort of.

A light came on. Oh, my word! How could she even move in there! Boxes piled to the ceiling. And was that a cradle in one corner? As much as I would like to have gone in there, the smell kept me back. I saw Alysha hold a tissue to her face, and Jan was mouth breathing. Frank didn't seem bothered but had set up the ladder and had the device installed one-two-three.

Today, Alysha's backbone was firmly in place. "Minnie. I'm sorry, but this room needs to be cleaned up. From now on, there will be a daily inspection until I'm satisfied you are not a health threat to this house. No argument or I will book a moving truck myself. In fact, I think I will arrange for a dumpster for this stuff to go in."

Minnie tried to sputter something, but Jan beat her to the punch. "That's two of us you'll need to fight on this. I'd suggest you choose your battles carefully."

"Living with a bunch of busy-bodies. Fine. But I'll do the cleaning myself. No one touches my things except me. Agreed?"

Alysha softened her tone, as she let Frank angle past her with the stepladder. "Agreed and thank you. I'll bring some garbage bags up and leave them outside your door."

She and Jan left the room, and both shook their heads at me. Message clear, no questions.

I'd see about that.

CHAPTER NINE
Alysha

Minnie's room was a shocker to me as I'd not realized the scope of the problem. Poor Dianne, living next to such a health hazard. I should have dealt with it long before now. I wondered about contacting her doctor for advice. There must be some explanation, and help, for the hoarding and the general filth.

No wonder there was a smell. We'd found rotting food scattered around the room. She must have raided the kitchen at times. Several potatoes had rotted to a black mushy pulp. And some cold cuts that hadn't been cold in a long time. I wasn't going to wait for her to toss those items. They went straight to a trash bag and out of there. Along with other unidentifiable food shapes, now covered with mould.

I dropped a dozen more garbage bags off at her room. Then I decided to head to the kitchen, to talk with Jan. We needed a plan to deal with the situation. We'd often discussed Minnie's obvious health issues, mental and otherwise.

Jan had a history with the Lodge. I reminisced about the time she told me about the love affair with my Uncle Dalton. It was a May - September union and they were very much in love. If they'd married, she would've been my aunt and owner of this place. I'd better not let Nina hear *that* story!

"Jan, are you there? Where is everybody this afternoon?"

I looked out the kitchen window to see Jan, standing with hands-on-hips, and glaring at Nina. Hemingway was racing around Jan's garden. Kicking up the dirt and digging. The garden was Jan's pride and joy. She provided all the vegetables for the Lodge from that plot. Another crisis. I needed to intervene before they killed each other.

"Ladies, what's all the shouting about? Here, Hemingway, good dog. Come!" To my surprise, the little terror obeyed. I scooped him up before he caused WWIII.

Jan fumed, her lips white with anger. I'd never seen her in such a state. As I drew nearer to her, I kept my voice calm. Not so easy when Nina's manner indicated her dog's behaviour should be considered normal.

I stood next to Jan. "Jan, I did say I would find somewhere for Hemingway to run. I'll speak to Frank and see what he suggests. Try to stay calm."

As if planned, Frank strolled out from the barn. "Oh, there he is now." I raised my voice. "Frank, over here. Need your help."

Frank waved and indicated he would be right there. I handed Hemingway, feet furiously paddling, to his owner. "Nina, you'd better wash him off. There's a tub in the mudroom, with some old towels."

"Of course. I do apologize for this little scallywag running all over your garden, Jan. But dogs will be dogs." She proceeded to pepper the dog's head with kisses. "Now we have to wash your tootsies, don't we?"

Jan exchanged a glance with me. No need for any eye rolls this time, from either of us. Then Jan's lips twitched ever so slightly when she spied the muddy paw prints down my shirt.

"Don't even go there," I said under my breath. "Have you calmed down now?"

Her shoulder shrug was all I got. The two women would never be the best of friends—Nina seemed oblivious to the upset she'd caused. And I knew how Jan felt about inconsiderate people. Neither of us had children, but I'd say we both believed that dogs, like children, needed boundaries.

Fortunately, Frank had now ambled up to us. He was one of the most pleasant people I knew and would be the perfect one to smooth choppy waters.

"Afternoon ladies. What can I do for you, Alysha? I heard all the ruckus from the barn." Then he realized there was a new face, and he visibly straightened. "Oh, pardon me. I don't think we've met."

I introduced him to Nina and his smile broadened. "Nice to meet you Miss, but I must warn you. Alpacas and dogs don't mix. If your pup was to go anywhere near them, he might get trampled. You'd not be happy about that would you?"

Before Nina could respond I decided to intervene. "Frank, perhaps you could make some sort of temporary run for Hemingway. You know, so he can exercise and do his business. That way he can't interfere with the alpacas or Jan's garden. Ms. Mikado is here for a few weeks to work on her new book. That should keep us all happy."

Frank listened to me but could not take his eyes off Nina. "Hemingway you say. One of my favourite writers. Not so popular these days. It's all that Grisham and Clancy stuff. Not for me."

Jan and I looked on in disbelief as Nina and Frank conversed about books. The two of us were now invisible. "I've become a Grisham fan lately, but I normally write cozies. I'm here, as Alysha has said, for a writing retreat and some research for my latest book. You know, true story, but written as fiction. There are stories everywhere."

Jan nudged me with her elbow as if to say *break this up*. Frank kept turning his hat in his hands, never taking his eyes off Nina, and had yet to acknowledge my request about a dog pen.

I cleared my throat. "Excuse me, Frank, do you think you could provide a small pen or run for the dog? The sooner the better, as we don't want to upset the pregnant alpacas. Right?"

The spell was broken. Frank turned away from Nina and faced me. "I'm sorry, Alysha, Ms. Mikado here looks so familiar to me. Perhaps I've read one of her books. I'll get started right away on a run for her wee Hemingway. I have some rolls of chicken wire and leftover wood. I'll ask Jeff to help, and we should have it by day's end."

"Thanks, Frank. Jan and I appreciate it."

Hemingway was now tucked under Nina's arm. It would seem the affection had limits—Nina didn't want dirt on her yellow scarf. She turned to walk away and gave a small wave to Frank. "Bath time for this dirty boy, and then I'm off to town. A few errands to run. Nice to meet you, Frank. He smiled at our writer guest who so far was nothing but trouble for the rest of us. He headed back to the barn, with a spring in his step and whistling a tune.

Jan, usually never at a loss for words, stood anchored in place as if she'd turned to stone.

"Earth to Jan—you okay? Let's get back inside. I'm in need of coffee."

She exhaled a pent-up breath, shook herself, and made eye contact with me. She nodded, and we walked back to the kitchen where she busied herself making coffee, without speaking a word. Her movements were deliberate and after she closed a cupboard door with a little more pressure than necessary, I urged her to sit down.

"Okay, another disaster averted. Frank will fix the problem with the dog, but what else has happened to upset you?"

"I'm sorry Alysha. I'm usually more in control of my feelings. I'm concerned at how agitated my parents are over Andrew's death. They're taking it harder than I would have imagined. Not so good at their age. And because they know Dax will keep me updated, they've been pestering me for information as well."

"But you haven't heard anything from him, right?"

"Not yet. I can't get them to understand how these things work. I know they're getting older, but they've always been better at coping with situations that are outside their control."

She offered up a small smile. "It's hard to see the roles changing."

I didn't have much experience with aging parents, so I couldn't offer any advice.

She continued. "When I speak with Dax, I may ask him to go and see them. It might have more impact if information comes from an *official* source. They'll know he has the same concerns for the young people."

"Sounds like a good idea, Jan."

Taking a deep breath, she stood and straightened her shoulders. I could see *housekeeper* Jan was back. She smiled at me. "Thanks for listening. It helps."

"Anytime."

"Now then, coffee's ready. I'll pour you a cup and then I need to get back to work. This place doesn't clean itself."

CHAPTER TEN
Dianne

It was early afternoon, and I was restless. I needed a shower after finally seeing the inside of Minnie's room. Made my skin crawl! I'm no Suzy Homemaker, but how could anyone live like that? I've seen episodes of those shows profiling hoarders, so I suppose I should be grateful her behaviour is limited to her room.

I hunted down Rose who was more than eager to head into town with me for a late lunch at one of the pubs.

Friday was a busy shopping day, so parking was at a premium. We decided on the Crossings Tavern but vetoed the patio considering the overcast sky. The rain wasn't finished yet, so we hurried to get inside.

Too late. I'd forgotten Cassie would be working here. Oh well, maybe we'd get preferred seats.

"Ladies! Nice to see you. Not wanting the patio, I guess?"

You think? "Inside's better for us today, thanks, Cassie."

"Follow me."

She seated us and pointed to the chalkboard listing the day's specials. Rose and I were happy to see fish and chips highlighted. We ordered and added a draft each to wash it down.

The pub was a favourite venue in town and always busy. Great pub grub and the bar did its best to highlight some of our local breweries with a varied selection of craft ales.

"Don't let me forget to pick up a bottle of tequila before we head back."

Rose laughed. "With or without the worm?"

"It's for Nina, so maybe the worm would be suitable?"

"She's quite the character, isn't she? And that dog!"

Further comments were put on hold as Cassie placed our meals in front of us. The beer was already going down a treat, and I was tempted to order another, but I was driving. What a pain being responsible is at times.

I sat facing the entrance, people watching is always entertaining. Rose was nattering on about something, but my attention was fixed with sickening clarity on the newest person to enter the bar. An attractive man, in his sixties, well dressed and accompanied by two other businessmen. They were laughing and not paying attention to the room. I ducked my head down and prayed he wouldn't look my way.

"Dianne Mitchell? What on earth are you doing here?"

My heart stopped. I lifted my head and met the puzzled look on Rose's face. It was brief because she instantly swiveled around to see who called my name.

Sloane Jackson. I thought I was done with him. I clenched my jaws to enforce a neutral look on my face. The less I said to him, the better.

He couldn't get over to our table fast enough. The nearer he got, the closer I was to throwing up. And there he stood. Arms open wide as if I was going to fall into them like Sleeping Beauty awakened by her Prince. Gag me.

"Dianne. It's me. Sloane."

My mouth had gone dry, and my palms were sweating. Extremes. That's always what Sloane did to me.

Rose twigged there was a problem, thank goodness. "I'm here, Dianne."

I gave her a brief nod and then faced the music. "I'd prefer to forget you, Sloane, but I'm busy, and have nothing to say to you."

"Still the kidder, I see. You look great by the way. What's it been? Five years? I knew I would find you eventually. You couldn't hide forever."

My appetite vanished, and I looked at my near-empty glass of beer. Drink it, or toss it at him?

Typical Sloane, he carried on, not paying mind to anything I said, and assuming I'd be overjoyed to see him. "If you live around here, we need to catch up. I can't today." He inclined his head toward his companions, who had found a table. "Business meeting. I've invested in that new restaurant and spa on the old mill property? Do you know it?" A frown displaced his near-perfect smile. "Now there's a police tie-up, and we've come to see what can be done to speed up the re-opening. I've rented a house along the river for a few days."

I was speechless and growing angry. I rummaged in my handbag for a few bills and tossed them on the table. "C'mon Rose. We need to leave, now."

She made no comment but stood and moved close to me. Waves of curiosity spilled from her. She'd have to wait.

"I repeat, Sloane. I have *nothing* to say to you. I don't want to see you." I had no control over my voice and couldn't believe I didn't care about what I said. I raised my voice for emphasis. "You can go to hell for all I care. More than one body's been found in that river. I'd be careful. Now, move out of my way."

Conversations all around us had stilled, and Cassie stood with a tray of drinks, rooted to the spot. Shit, this would be all over the lodge before the end of the day. I'd deal with it later.

I grabbed Rose's arm and we hightailed it out of there, ignoring the looks, and not saying a word. I was shaking so bad, I almost tripped over my own feet. I knew Rose had a million questions - who wouldn't - but I was grateful she didn't voice them. She did voice genuine concern. "Breathe, Dianne, breathe. Do you want to go to your car, or find someplace to sit?"

I pointed up the street to the *Java Hut*. "In there."

We hustled inside and found a table away from the windows. I collapsed onto a chair while Rose went to the counter for a couple of coffees.

Sloane bloody Jackson. I thought I'd seen the last of him. How much to tell Rose was my next problem. If I was going to spill the whole story, I'd rather it was to Jan and even Alysha. Rose would get the condensed version.

She placed a coffee in front of me. "Here you go. It's too bad Cassie was there. You know the whole house will hear about this in short order?"

I nodded as I brought the brew to my lips. The shaking had subsided, but the memories hadn't.

"I guess you'd like an explanation?" That was like asking if a car needed gas to run.

"Only what you want to share." The eager look on her face told me she'd be more than happy to hear *everything*. Wasn't going to happen.

I mentally sighed. "His name's Sloane Jackson. I met him a long time ago where I used to work back in Toronto. He was interested in me, which was fine at first. But then not so much. Without going into details, let's say moving here to Grant's Crossing was a means to get away from him and disappear out of his life."

Rose narrowed her eyes. Of course, she wanted more, but I was disinclined to share. She reached her hand across the table and patted mine. "Water under the bridge, am I right? Not too many of us have completely escaped a distasteful romance."

A distasteful romance? Sure, that's one way to describe it, and I didn't correct her.

"Do you think he would show up at the house?"

Oh, god. My stomach lurched at the thought. "I hope not. But you could be right. I think we'd better get back there. I should give Jan and Alysha the heads up."

"Well, he'll get no welcome from me, count on it!"

I thanked her, and we left. I remembered I had one thing on my to-do list, and before we returned to the car, I ducked into the liquor store. I felt furtive, sure that Sloane would suddenly appear again.

With the promised bottle of tequila in hand, we headed back to the lodge.

As we came into the house, Rose promised, again, she wouldn't say a word. I figured she wouldn't have to. We parted ways and I headed to the kitchen, where Jan was beginning preparation for our casual Friday evening meal.

She was slicing cold leftover chicken. I could see boxes of crackers and cut-up cheese, along with pickles and other condiments.

"Can I give you a hand?"

Jan turned and wiped her hands on a towel. "Dianne." She eyed my purchase. "Ah, a supplement for the cart? Or personal use?"

I held up the bottle. "Our writer friend indicated a preference. I thought I would be sociable."

Jan smiled, and then she looked at me. "Are you okay? You look like you've seen a ghost."

I took a breath. "You could say that. And I'd rather you hear it from me first. A bit of an incident just now in the tavern, and of course Cassie saw it all."

"I understand. She'll be bursting with whatever she saw by the time she returns Sunday, I assume?"

"I'll be lucky if she doesn't talk to a Gazette reporter or CNN!" I tried to make light of it but wasn't having much success.

Jan pulled out a chair. "Sit." She handed me a glass of water and waited.

"His name is Sloane Jackson. Met him years ago where I worked. He took a shine to me. Successful businessman, a little flashy, but could show me a good time. At first, it was all too perfect, and I began to think it might get serious. But then he started getting weird. Enjoyed being in control - over me - with all the earmarks of a jealous streak. Started wanting to know where I was every minute I wasn't with him. You know?"

"A familiar story, Dianne. Sad but true. Did he ever hurt you?"

The tears spilled. I couldn't stop them.

"Oh, no!" She grabbed a tissue and handed me several. "You don't have to tell me if you don't want to." Then she glanced toward the kitchen door. "Sorry, not a good time, Nina. Can you take Hemingway out the front door this time, please?"

Damn. Nina was the last person who needed to know anything about this. I clammed up and let Jan do her thing.

"Sorry to interrupt, ladies. Is there anything I can do to help? Hemingway here is always a good comfort to me when I'm upset. So intuitive, dogs are."

"Not this time, Nina, if you don't mind." Jan moved toward her, and Nina got the hint. Jan stood watching her leave and didn't turn back to me until she heard the front door close. "Sorry about that, Dianne. Go on if you like."

Without a word, I pulled my blouse away from my shoulder. Jan shut her eyes and flinched at the cigarette burns she saw. "Oh, Dianne. I'm so sorry."

"Yeah. Me too." The weepy tears had gone and once again anger at what he'd done to me reared its ugly head. "It was the one, and only, time he hurt me. Physically at least. No way I'd give him a second chance. Ty had been bugging me to come and stay here, and I'd never mentioned it to Sloane, so I disappeared. Quit my job without notice and left no forwarding address. Chickening out I guess, but I just needed to run."

"Ah. So not the early retirement you told us?" Jan didn't say anything else for a moment but shook her head from side to side. "Men can be such brutes." Then I saw her put the pieces together. "Wait! He's here? In Grant's Crossing?"

"Nailed it. Bastard saw me, with Rose. Acted as if nothing had ever happened, as if he could pick up where we left off. He's staying in town for a few days. Believe it or not, he has business ties to the new spa and resort. Irony or what? He could show up here. Which is why I'm telling you."

Jan's mouth tightened, and her eyes flashed. "He won't step a foot inside this house - I promise you. We need to tell Alysha."

"Yes, I agree. As for the others, well Cassie's talents will see to that. But no one else needs to know all the details. Other than a relationship that ended and is *not* going to be resurrected!"

As is often the case, talking about demons lessens their hold, and I thanked Jan. She responded by asking for help emptying the dishwasher and setting out plates for dinner. It would be a welcome distraction. I washed my hands and set to work.

We worked together and made note of Jeff helping Frank with the construction of a dog run for Hemingway. Through the kitchen window, we could see Nina had engaged them in a lively discussion - probably about me.

Jan nudged me. "I'd say there'll be lots to discuss at dinner this evening."

"What have I missed?" Alysha had come into the kitchen unnoticed, and I turned with a start.

"Dianne, I can finish up here, if you want to have a chat with Alysha before dinner."

"Okay, I will, thanks. Let's go for a walk, Alysha."

She wore a puzzled look but didn't miss a beat. We headed outside, but away from the direction of Nina and her audience. No need for them to overhear any of this. Finding a quiet and shady spot, we sat on one of several benches scattered on the grounds.

Without preamble, I repeated to Alysha what I'd told Jan. Poor kid. Judging by the look on her face, domestic abuse was something she'd only heard about, and - fortunately - had no first-hand knowledge. Her close call with Ty, though, gave her all the ammunition she needed.

Her expression was serious. "I agree with Jan and will do whatever it takes to ensure Mr. Jackson never shows his face around here. We've fended off a news crew, right? And I dealt with Ty - so we can handle the likes of Sloane Jackson. No matter what!"

CHAPTER ELEVEN
Alysha

With no specific chores, Saturdays had become my best day of the week. Jan and Cassie alternate weekends away so meals are less formal. This was Cassie's weekend off, leaving Jan in charge of meals. Brilliant. It's no secret, most of us prefer her down-to-earth cooking over Cassie's trends. As for me, I hoped to find time, and a noise-free space, to work on my real estate plans. I had lots of ideas and was excited about my career prospects. After being at Leven Lodge for a year, I felt settled in its routines and could step back a little for my own interests.

Yesterday's stormy weather was history, and the sky was a cloudless blue. Jeff loved to barbecue—tonight would be perfect for it and would give Jan a break. He was at home working the grill. I think he enjoys being the centre of attention, but I won't argue if it provides a change of pace.

Barbecue - eating outside, right. I'd need to remind Nina it would still mean Hemingway had to be kept out of sight. She'd only been here two days and it already felt like a week.

I lingered longer than usual to enjoy my coffee on the balcony. The air was fresh, and songbirds greeted the day. I started ticking things off my to-do list until I remembered what I'd heard from Dianne last night.

I sat back in my chair. What she'd told me had disturbed me more than I thought it would. Maybe I'd become more sensitive to physical assaults after last year, or maybe I was growing up. I backed Dianne completely and admired her fortitude to get out of a toxic relationship. Although, it pissed me off that it always seemed to be the victim who had to run, and there wasn't necessarily justice for the assailant. Waiting for *karma* wasn't always an option.

She'd come here to find an oasis of safety, and I was determined this home would always provide it for all who lived here. Jan set the standards where that was concerned. She bolstered the atmosphere my grandmother had established. So, I'd need to be on guard if he were to show up. I'd shared a little of the story with Jeff, but only Jan and I had Dianne's full confidence. No one else needed to know the details, and we certainly had no desire to have Nina speculating on how to turn Dianne's life into one of her books.

My shoulders had tensed with my mind's wanderings, and I had to make the effort to loosen up. I added a note to my to-do list about the possibility of installing security cameras. Probably wouldn't be a bad idea to have some down by the barn as well. I imagined teasing Jeff that I'd always have an eye on him.

One last look out over the fields and I drained my coffee mug. Jeff would be busy with the alpacas and other odds and ends. And I reluctantly prodded myself to see how Minnie's room cleaning efforts were progressing. Jeff had offered to move boxes or take stuff to the dump. I'm beginning to think he might hold a soft spot for her!

I took to the stairs and found Jan setting up a pastry-laden tray for our light breakfast.

"Mornin', Jan. I came to give you some help. What can I do?"

She laid the last danish on the tray and looked up with a smile. "Thanks, Alysha. If you want to take this tray through, I'll top up the coffee. Have to keep the hungry hordes happy."

I laughed. "That's a lot of alliteration for first thing in the morning."

"And without even trying," she chuckled, not missing a beat.

I was still smiling as I made an appearance in the dining room and set out the tray next to a selection of fresh fruit. Other than Nina, everyone was there.

"Are you sitting with us this morning, Alysha, dear?" Rose asked, grabbing a pastry before I'd barely moved my hands away.

"In a little bit, maybe. Don't wait on me, I'm helping Jan in the kitchen. Just wanted to say good morning. How about a barbecue today? I'll order something tasty from the butcher and Jeff can work his magic."

As I expected, the suggestion was met with positive reactions all around.

"I take it that's a yes. Let's meet on the veranda at five for the usual cocktail hour. Philip looked up from his book. "The word grill is often used for barbecue, but a barbecue is not always a grill. By that I mean, a grill can be used indoors or out, but a barbecue must only be used outside."

"Um, okay, thanks for that, Philip." I saw Minnie's mouth working and kept talking to head her off. "I'm sure Jeff is well aware of the difference, and we'll all enjoy a great meal this evening. Isn't that right, Minnie?"

Success. I deflated her, and she threw me a sullen look. "So now if you'll all excuse me, I'll get back to the kitchen. Leave some food for Nina, please."

I returned to the kitchen and found Jan on the phone.

"I understand, Dax. Thank you."

His call was short, but not so sweet, according to Jan. "He's off duty today and will drop by to give us an update. They've brought in a more senior detective to handle *issues* in Grants Crossing." Her brow wrinkled. "Dax is not amused by this turn of events, as someone from the city is not always aware of how things are managed here."

"Oh, Jan, try not to worry so much. Sometimes we need to leave it to the experts. Dax knows how these things work."

Jan grinned at me, "Listen to you, giving out advice." She inclined her head toward the dining room. No surprise to hear one voice raised above the others. "Maybe as an expert yourself on Minnie you should get back there and keep the peace before the writer arrives."

I gave a mock bow and turned to leave.

"I'll let you know when Dax shows up." She paused as if weighing her next words. "You know he enjoys your company."

I turned back to her. Where did that comment come from? "What does that mean, exactly?"

"It's no secret, to me, that he has an interest in you. You're blushing!"

"I certainly am not." I needed to change the subject, fast. "I just told the others that Jeff will barbecue tonight - can you order enough steaks? He'll bake the potatoes as well. You only need to worry about side dishes and dessert, please and thanks."

Her eyes twinkled. "I'll put the order in. Maybe I should extra and invite Dax?"

Although I knew she was teasing, I decided not to respond and headed back to the dining room.

Nina, with her usual flair for making a late entrance, had just arrived. Instinctively I turned my attention towards Minnie. Looked like she'd been haranguing Lily over something. Poor Lily wore her hang-dog expression and listlessly pushed the remnants of food around on her plate. But here was a better target for sharp-shooting Minnie.

Nina wore a yellow sundress. Retro style, with a flared skirt and a bodice, held up by two wide straps of fabric knotted in a bow behind her neck. Rose's eyes lit up. She was a dress designer by trade and had an eye for detail. To me, the dress made me think of old photos I'd seen of Marilyn Munroe.

Nina flashed a smile as bright as her dress. "Good morning one and all. Everyone chipper today?" I don't think she expected an answer because she didn't miss a beat but headed to the remains of breakfast on the sideboard. "Chipper, and hungry by the looks of what's left! I'll just take this last lonely danish and some fruit."

To no one's surprise, Nina proved to be new material for Minnie. "You're the only one *chipper* around here this morning. And looks like your poodle is missing." She pointed to Nina's dress.

Dianne stifled a giggle. And I had to bite my lip, as images of those fifties' poodle skirts flashed across my mind.

Nina was either oblivious to the reference or chose to ignore it. "Speaking of Hemingway, Minnie dear, he's quite intrigued with your cast-offs. Is this a yearly event, or long overdue?" She nibbled on the danish. "Oh, sorry, perhaps they're treasures? In any event, I'll try not to trip over the stuff piled in the hall."

"The dog looks more like a rat! It best stay far away from me. I pay good money for privacy around here. I might be overpaying this month."

"If I were you, Minnie, I wouldn't rock the boat about your accommodation. This is such a lovely place to call home."

"And if I were you, I wouldn't go out in the daylight!"

All eyes focused on Minnie and her less than subtle attack at Nina.

Ignoring her taunt, Nina smiled at one and all. "How kind of you to mention Hemingway—I'll pass on your regards. As we speak, he's enjoying the charming run that handsome handyman, Frank, built."

At the mention of Frank, Minnie sucked air through her teeth. She glowered at Nina. "You know nothing about Frank!"

Minnie, speaking up for Frank? What was behind that? Nina let the comment slide and finished her observation. "Oh, and with help, of course, from your man, Alysha.

I would not let her get under my skin! *My man*, indeed! I mean, he is my man, but the way she spoke made me cringe.

As if on cue Jeff entered the dining room and offered the perfect distraction. "I heard through the grapevine that a barbecue is needed this evening. So, everyone attending? Nina, I do a medium-rare that is to die for - so I've been told."

All heads turned in her direction. Breaking out in a smile meant for *only Jeff*, she simply said, "I can't wait."

Oh boy, maybe we'd better keep the tequila hidden.

CHAPTER TWELVE
Dianne

Jessica Fletcher should take up residence. Grant's Crossing was in danger of becoming Cabot's Cove North. Two murders last year and now another potential one?

The sultry July afternoon had brought everyone, except Minnie, outside to find a shady spot on the veranda. Book for Philip, a game of cribbage for Rose and Lily. Nina sat, with Hemingway snoozing at her feet, off to one side, as if to observe. Her laptop sat open on the small table near her.

The boisterous tongue-wagging heard earlier, would work up appetites for food, and gossip, among the group. There'd be no Gazette until Monday morning, so if we needed details on the body found, we'd have to wait. Unless Jan's nephew had news.

In the meantime, I had other matters on my mind. Sloane. I'd barely slept the previous night. My thoughts ran from feeling sick about seeing him again to outright anger that I'd allowed him to have the influence he did on my life. Part of me wanted to hide out until he'd left the area, but that would mark me a coward.

I'd never let anyone know why I'd left Toronto in such a hurry. Ty, of course, had known and had been part of his motivation to bring me here. He'd laid the groundwork for my retirement angle. But now I reconsidered his motivation. You know, when you think you know someone and then you find out otherwise, it makes you doubt everything you thought about them. Aaargh. More anger to fuel me.

I'd let my mind wander because when I focused back on reality, an atmosphere of tension had taken over our peaceful setting with

Minnie's arrival. Nina's fingers were poised over the keyboard—ready to record a juicy tidbit?

Minnie was worked up about something, and Alysha had taken her aside. While Alysha kept her voice low, Minnie didn't care.

"Dog pee! Do something, Alysha, or I will!"

Eyes flew in Nina's direction. Hemingway had come to attention, quivering as if ready to attack. Alysha tried to placate Minnie, but it wasn't happening. She pushed Alysha aside and stomped over to Nina. The dog was on full alert, yapping and straining to bite at Minnie's bony ankle. Nina scooped the dog up and kept a cool manner. "Problem, Minnie?"

"You bet your ass there's a problem. Came out of my room just now and nearly slipped in a puddle of that thing's pee. What are you going to do about it?"

"Oh, dear. Of course, I'll go and wipe it up. I'm sorry. Hemingway sometimes can't wait until we get down all those stairs. Weak bladder. You can probably relate."

Minnie's cheeks turned red. Alysha rushed over. "Please, ladies. Let's get this sorted out before anything else is said."

Nina had to be fully aware of riling a hornet's nest, but played it cool, while still delivering a dig. "Hemingway, let's go and clean up your little accident. Mummy's not angry, but you've upset our friend."

Minnie continued to glare as Nina left, and muttered, "She's no friend of mine! That woman is a walking migraine. Wish I had a pill to make her disappear."

The drama had ended, for now. But Alysha still had Minnie to deal with. "I am sorry, Minnie, about the dog. But they're only here for a few weeks. And once you have your room cleaned up and all the, ah, discarded items removed, I'd think the situation with the dog will improve."

"Estelle would have handled this."

Alysha's tone turned stern. "My grandmother's not here, Minnie. So, like it or not, I'm the one in charge. And speaking of your room, I'm heading up there now to see what progress has been made. No - you stay here, and cool down."

Minnie skulked to one end of the veranda, rummaged around in her knitting bag, and pulled out her latest project. She kept muttering to herself as the needles began to click with a furious beat. Best to let her settle down by herself.

Philip had gone back to reading, and the twins wisely let the sleeping dog - I mean Minnie - lie. With some surprise, I realized I'd enjoyed the reprieve from my own drama.

I sat reflecting on the day for almost half an hour until I noticed Minnie quietly pack up her knitting and move inside the house. My curiosity took over. And I decided to follow.

I let her have the advantage of heading upstairs first. She took the elevator, and after a minute I began climbing the stairs.

Boxes and bags had accumulated outside the elevator door. Odd bits of furniture had also been scraped along the hallway floor from Minnie's room. Wonders would never cease. The old bat was doing as she'd been told.

Alysha and Nina were nowhere in sight, so I assumed Hemingway's mishap had been remedied.

Maybe Minnie could do with a helping hand?

Her door was partly open. I didn't know if the chaos I saw was new or her usual décor. A small path had been cleared from the doorway to the window. I could see an old rocking chair, next to the small wooden cradle I'd seen earlier. The rocking chair had the only available space for sitting. Piles of clothes, and balls of yarn, covered Minnie's bed. Every available surface had knick-knacks or books strewn about.

She was off in one corner, her back to me. And she was murmuring to herself. I couldn't make out what she was saying. I knocked on the door frame. "Need help with anything?"

I must have startled her. She wheeled around so fast; a stray bobby pin dropped to the ground. Her wiry hair threatened to escape the remainder of the pins. Her eyes reminded me of a cornered raccoon I'd seen once. Frightened, but ready to attack. I backed up a couple of steps. "Sorry. Just thought I'd ask." Why was I apologizing, and more importantly what had I been thinking?

"Get out, get out!" She scuttled toward me; her witchy hands headed for my face. Didn't have to tell me twice. I wasn't going to run even though I wanted to.

The door slammed behind me, and I realized I was shaking. She had scared the bejeebers out of me. A quick look around meant my cowardly secret was safe from inquisitive eyes. Then, I casually walked down the hall to my room, where I finally calmed myself.

And then it was time to freshen up for Jeff's barbecue. I looked forward to his expertise with the grill. He seemed to enjoy himself and knew how to cook a perfect steak.

If I was lucky, I'd enjoy good conversation and a fine meal and could keep thoughts of Sloane Jackson at bay. *If* I was lucky.

CHAPTER THIRTEEN
Alysha

Most Saturday evenings Jeff and I headed to town and enjoyed a game of darts with friends at one of the local pubs. This Saturday, though, the pubs would likely be filled with speculation over the recent death that was making news in town. I wasn't fond of gossip, so having a barbecue with the residents this evening had much more appeal.

Besides if I needed gossip, there was more than enough on hand right here. Minnie could be annoying, but I agreed with her about the dog's accident outside her door. I'd checked in on her a couple of hours ago to see how she was progressing with her room clean-up. Depressing scene, and slow going. But at least the horrible odours had lessened. I'd encouraged her to make use of air fresheners - but no candles! For someone as frenetic as her, she worked at a snail's pace on this. I'd need to find something to motivate her. Maybe Jeff would succeed where others failed. He had a way with the ladies, even her.

I hoped she'd be a little more mellow at dinner and vowed to keep her away from Nina. She's competing with Minnie in rubbing me the wrong way. That made me chuckle. Should I tell them they have something in common?

Dianne had kept to herself most of the day, but of course, she'd been on hand to witness the sparring match between Minnie and Nina over Hemingway. This business with Sloane Jackson must be playing on her because I'd been surprised she hadn't let loose a couple of comments to either Minnie or Nina. Proper vetting of future residents was a priority - no matter how long they stayed.

All these thoughts ran through my mind as I splashed water on my face and tamed my curls. Along with those thoughts was a rising tide of irritation that I hadn't been able to spend five minutes on my real estate paperwork. At least, this year, I wasn't involved with another suspicious death! The thought of more crime on the grounds of property my family used to own, made me shiver.

I stared at my reflection in the mirror. I'd surprised myself since coming to Grant's Crossing with how much I'd changed. The Grants had a long history of adversity since coming from Scotland nearly two hundred years ago. I thought of the transom window above the front door. It held the Grant crest. *Stand Fast.* I laughed at myself. I'd been a stubborn one growing up, so *Stand Fast* could have been written for me.

Changing into a cotton summer dress out of my usual shorts and tee, completed my attempts to spruce up. Jeff would say I cleaned up well. Jeff. If I could only get him to see how much I needed proper time to develop my real estate goals. I didn't complain about all the time he spent with the alpacas, did I? He needed a nudge back in my direction.

There. I had a plan and I'd discuss this with him later.

I ran down the stairs, feeling more lighthearted than earlier, and headed to the garden. Strands of fairy lights had been strung through the shrubbery and when it grew dark, would bathe the garden in a magical light.

Jeff stood over the barbecue, checking gas levels and the cleanliness of the grill. He hadn't seen me arrive, so I crept up behind him and circled my arms around his waist. "Need any help?"

He turned and kissed me. "You smell nice. I appreciate the offer, babe, but your help's not needed. Jan and I are a team tonight."

"Are you now? Should I be jealous?" I was in the mood to tease.

"No, I don't think so, but the shoe will be on the other foot when your admirer arrives. Not only do you smell fantastic, but you look so pretty tonight. Is this for him?"

I stood back from him so I could see his face better. "What are you talking about? Who do you mean?"

"Didn't Jan tell you she'd invited Dax Young to the barbecue, that able young detective who took a shine to you last year?"

I turned away to hide my blushing. It's true that DC Young flirted with me last year when he led the investigation into events at Leven Lodge, and Ty Rogers' criminal activity. I most certainly didn't encourage him.

Saved by the bell. I was about to answer Jeff with some trite retort when the gang arrived. Dianne went straight to the bar cart that had been brought out to the garden. I was relieved to see she looked rested and showed no signs of anxiety.

"Who would like a cocktail or a soda? Whatever your poison. Aha, I see we have some tequila for Nina." Dianne brandished the bottle in Nina's direction. "Not sure if we have the right mixes for this, so I'll let you serve yourself."

Before Nina could respond, a voice broke into the conversation. A voice that immediately brought me back to a police investigation. "Let me do the honours. I see some orange juice and soda. Perfect. Tequila Sunrise anyone?"

Detective Constable Dax Young was a handsome man. He had an air of confidence about him that let me think he probably knew it. He towered over me at six feet and more. Perfect build for a police officer. Clean-shaven, his dark hair was slicked back. And his probing eyes had zeroed in on me. He wore no working suit today but had dressed down for the barbecue. Did I mention an air of confidence? Bordering on arrogant, in my opinion, but I guess that's good in a detective. He smiled at the assembled group, but his eyes never left mine. Jeff called out a greeting and offered him a beer.

I'll pass on the beer, thanks, Jeff." He finally broke eye contact, and I felt guilty. Why?

He brought all the ingredients together and asked for takers on the Tequila Sunrise. "It's my specialty.

Nina was full of surprises, including an as yet unheard, sultry voice. "Right up my alley, sweet cheeks. Say, are you our official bartender for the evening? I tip well if you are."

For once I'd be happy to give the spotlight to Nina. I let Jeff introduce them. "Nina, meet Jan's nephew, Dax Young. Or Detective Constable Young when he's on duty."

Nina giggled. "So, I'd better not drink and drive, should I, officer?"

Oh, come on, Dianne, say something! Dax lapped up the comments like a cat with spilled cream.

Dianne moved forward; hand outstretched to take one of the cocktails. "Nina don't put our *young* detective in an awkward situation. I'm sure you've years and *years* of driving experience to know better."

The age dig scored a point with Minnie, who only snickered and thankfully didn't add any comments of her own.

"Seems to be a popular drink this evening. Might need some more *juice*." Dax had deflected the drinking and driving commentary. But Nina had winked at the juice reference.

Jan came out to the garden carrying a tray loaded with salads and rolls. "And when did you become such an expert in the cocktail department?"

"You don't know *everything* about me, Aunt Jan. You're just in time to observe my skill as a bartender—in case my career with the force doesn't work out."

Jan cast a baleful eye at her nephew. "If you say so. Is there anything else you need before we eat?"

"Maybe more orange juice if the ladies want another."

Nina piped up and purred. "Yes, please."

Philip kept reading and paid no attention, while Minnie glared at Jeff as if to say, "Hurry up with my steak. I've had enough with these fools and their fancy drinks."

***

Another successful barbecue with steaks grilled to perfection! And by the looks on faces all around, I think Jeff had passed the grade once again. We sat, side by side, empty plates pushed away. I was about to congratulate my guy on a job well done when a hand tapped me on the shoulder.

"Alysha, can I have a word?" Dax's hand on my shoulder lingered a little too long for my taste, but I didn't want to appear rude by drawing attention to it.

"Sure, Dax. What's up?" Oh, those eyes! Like they could see right through me. "Did you want something else to eat? There's not much left over."

"No, thanks. The meal was excellent by the way, Jeff. You are the grill master of Leven Lodge."

The smile on Jeff's face left no doubt he agreed with Dax's compliment. And then Dax's attention returned to me.

"I have an update on the body found at the mill. Thought you might be interested. But maybe we could get away from prying eyes and ears?"

Why on earth did his question make me feel uncomfortable? Was it the undertone to his voice? An update, yes. But the implication we move away from the group bothered me. I struck a compromise. "Yes, and I'm sure Jan would want to hear as well. She's back in the kitchen. Let's go find her, okay?"

His face fell for a moment, but he regrouped. "Yes, if you prefer. Good idea."

We walked back to the house. I don't think he understood the meaning of personal space because he sure kept crowding mine.

And then he reached for my arm, causing us to stop walking. Now what?

"By the way, I heard you're searching for a real estate broker in the area, to gain some experience?"

While I was unnerved he seemed to know so much about me, I couldn't pass up a potential business opportunity. "Yes, that's true. Do you have a lead?"

"I just might know of someone. If you give me your phone number, I'll text you the information later."

Trapped. I reluctantly gave him my number. Well, he was the police after all and I guessed he could find it out anyway if he really wanted. We continued on our way to the house.

I was relieved to see Jan hard at work dishing up bowls of strawberries and cream. She looked up as we approached.

"Hi, you two. Just in time to help me bring dessert outside. Hope folks have left some room - these beautiful strawberries won't last another day."

"Be glad to help, Jan. But first, Dax has some news he wants to share."

"About Andrew Makwa, Aunt Jan."

She was all ears and put down the spoon. "Please tell me there is something I can share with his grandparents, Dax. Unless they already know? They and their friends are distraught. They dislike the feeling of being kept in the dark as to what happened. As do I."

Dax perched himself on the edge of the kitchen table much to Jan's chagrin. He didn't speak for a few minutes as if gathering his thoughts. Then he turned and smiled at me. I was mentally phrasing a polite, but firm, way to bring a halt to his blatant flirting. Although, it's not bad for the ego.

Jan's expression bordered on impatience. "This dessert needs to be served soon! So out with it. If you have news, Dax, spit it out!"

He leaned forward and stole a strawberry from one of the plates. His playful expression was temporary, soon replaced with a serious manner.

"You can relax, Aunt Jan. Andrew's parents have been informed and this is a courtesy, of sorts, because of your standing with the family. It shouldn't be shared with anyone else, though. Understood?"

Not sharing police news with anyone else. Suddenly I was back in time when I'd first met DC Young and he'd taken me aside with confidential news about the McTaggart's estranged daughter, Janet. I wasn't sure I enjoyed this exclusive status. But I held my tongue and let him continue.

"I think I told you a senior Inspector from the crime unit in Toronto has been called in to head up this inquiry. It's no real secret there's been an increase in crime, mostly drug-related, since last year's murders, and your own close call, Alysha. You have to appreciate I can't go into details, but we believe young Andrew's death was a drug deal gone bad."

"What can I tell his parents, Dax? Has anyone been caught yet?"

"Not yet. We have one or two on our radar. These things don't get solved like on TV, you know. Our liaison officer has been in touch with the Makwa family to keep them updated and will continue to do so."

Jan touched his arm. "I'm not upset with you, Dax. It's just harder when you know the family of a victim. I feel helpless. Like I'm letting them down."

He flashed a genuine smile of empathy, unlike his earlier expressions of over-confidence. "You know I work with the youth on the reserve and coach the lacrosse team. They're a good group of guys but there's always a bad apple in every basket. Social media influences are powerful, the need to fit in, to not be seen as different. Kids have so much more pressure than I did at their age. They're too damn vulnerable. And I wish I could do more."

A genuine passion for kids came through loud and clear and caused me to see him in a better light. We don't always show all facets of our lives at once.

"I appreciate what you've been able to share, and I don't want you to feel I'm pressuring you, but..."

He played into her lighter tone and smiled. "But what?" Dax knew how to turn on the charm, and I was glad he'd directed it at Jan, and not me. I wondered why I was even in on this conversation at all. Made me think he hadn't wanted to talk with Jan at all, but only with me. I needed to focus on the teasing look on Jan's face.

"DC Young, can you tell us if the spa and restaurant are to be opened to the public anytime soon? Asking for a friend."

"Indeed, Ms. Young. You and your *friend* will be happy to know the tape is coming down tomorrow and business should resume as normal on Monday. I'm sure the Gazette will have all the details."

The mood was light-hearted, and we could hear voices and laughter from the garden. Nina's was distinct and loud. If the tequila bottle was empty, I wouldn't be replacing it.

I started putting dessert bowls on trays. "We'd best get this out there now before the party breaks up."

***

Despite Minnie's usual anti-social behaviour and my brief interruption with Dax's news, we experienced a pleasant meal and conversations under a warm summer's sky. Everyone seemed at ease. Or just the effects of full stomachs perhaps. A truce, of sorts, appeared to be in place between Minnie and Nina. Jeff loved to entertain, theatrically at times, with numerous jokes and stories. Even a tale or two about the alpacas - shocking surprise. Lots of fun, but he'd better not expect to be compensated as the evening's entertainment - at least not monetarily.

Not long after the meal ended, Philip took his leave. Conversational small talk wasn't his style. And then Minnie up and left as well. True to form, she pocketed a couple of buttered dinner rolls and didn't care that I'd seen her. She waltzed past me on the way to the barn, muttering something about preferring Frank's sensible company. We'd invited Frank to the meal, but he declined, saying he'd eaten earlier.

I'd learned that she and Frank had a history, of sorts. She'd known him since coming to Grant's Crossing, eons ago. According to Jan, she was never unpleasant to him - what an honour! And he must see something we're missing because he's only ever been kind, gentle, and patient with her. More than once, Frank had been enlisted to calm her down. When he was around her, she almost seemed human. Not an ounce of nastiness. There had to be a story there.

Dusk had settled and the summer evening had a stillness that was so peaceful. Rose, our avid flower expert, had been schooling me in some of the plants that graced the property. I detected the faint scent of almonds that belonged to a mass of purple heliotrope in a nearby flower bed. I secretly hoped I'd inherited Gran's green thumb. She had loved her roses. I smiled to myself at the memories conjured up.

The barbecue was all but done for another day, and coffee was offered to those who wished. Count me in, of course! I can drink it five minutes before bed and still sleep quite fine, thank you.

I closed my eyes for a moment to savour the restful atmosphere, content with how the day was winding down.

The crunch of wheels on gravel interrupted my quietude and I opened my eyes with some reluctance to see Jeff and Dax's attention taken with an approaching vehicle. Not just any vehicle, but a late-model Mercedes.

The car came to a stop, headlights doused, and the door opened. As the well-dressed stranger emerged, red flags went up. I glanced at Jan as my sixth sense kicked in. I just *knew* who had arrived on our doorstep.

CHAPTER FOURTEEN
Dianne

The delicious steak I'd enjoyed became a rock in my stomach. What the hell was he doing here? Whoever gave him my address was no friend of mine.

He moved toward me. At the same time, Alysha and Jan did likewise, placing themselves on either side of me.

Thankfully Minnie had already left. As had Philip. Rose was on alert, and from the corner of my eye, I saw Dax lay a hand on Jeff's arm. Gentle restraint.

I wouldn't be so nice.

"Dianne, sweetheart. Introduce me to your friends." His smile was as insincere as his behaviour. He turned to face everyone. "I'm not interrupting a special occasion, am I?"

Anger, like molten lava, bubbled up inside me. "I thought I made it clear to you I don't want to see you. Ever!"

"Come, come, Dianne. I'm willing to let bygones be bygones." He opened his arms for a hug.

Are you freaking kidding me! I swatted at his nearest arm. "Get lost, Sloane! My friends here know all about you, so you can drop the nice guy act." I'd leave the fact there was a cop on hand as a last resort.

"You must be Sloane Jackson." Jan's tone was all business. "I'm going to ask you to leave this property. It's abundantly clear you're not welcome."

Typical Sloane. His pretentious manner came to the fore. How had I once ever found him attractive? He extended a hand toward Jan. "And you must be Ms. Young. You're the maid here I believe."

Alysha bristled and moved forward. "You can address any questions to me, Mr. Jackson. I'm Alysha Grant, owner of this property. But as *Ms. Young* has stated, you are not welcome here and I would like you to leave. Now."

My breathing was laboured and blood pounded in my head. Fight or flight - that's what adrenaline does. I couldn't decide what I wanted to do more. I was beyond indignation and starting to see red.

I stepped ahead of Jan and Alysha and struggled to keep my voice calm. Icy calm. "Would you like me to show all these good people how much you *loved* me?" I began to pull at my top. "I could just kill you for what you did to me. For how you made me feel. Frightened by my own shadow, you bastard!"

He stepped back and the enthusiasm of his earlier greeting toned down. "That won't be necessary. I can see this is neither the time nor place for us to have a conversation about our relationship."

I exploded. "There is *no* relationship, you self-centered, conceited, son of a bitch! Get lost. If you died tomorrow, I wouldn't shed a tear."

Lily's gasp was true to form, but I didn't turn to look at her. Rose could take care of her. But then a rush of air preceded Nina's march to the scene. Sloane nearly stumbled backward, and I was ecstatic to see his composure falter.

She was in his face before he could catch his breath. "I know the likes of you, mister. Think you're a big man and all that. You're nothing but a cowardly slug. All dressed up but can't hide the rot underneath. You heard these ladies - get lost!"

I started shaking and felt a hand on my shoulder. Dax. He gently steered me to stand behind him. Jan put an arm around me, and Alysha grabbed my hand.

"Sir, I think these ladies have made it crystal clear you are to leave. I'm Detective Constable Dakotah Young, and my aunt to whom you referred a moment ago is *not* the maid of this house. I will not dignify this conversation with any more explanation. But if you do not immediately get in your vehicle and drive away, you will be charged with trespassing. And if Ms. Mitchell wishes, I can see to assault charges being laid."

Sloane's overbearing attitude had returned, but at least he knew when to call it quits. "This isn't over, Dianne. Unresolved issues. I'll see you around town, *sweetheart*."

He turned back to his car. Before he unlocked the door, he opened a pack of cigarettes and with deliberate movement, lit one keeping his eyes on me. "Later, my love."

Then he was gone, and I could breathe again.

I was surrounded by concern. My knees turned to water and Alysha pulled a lawn chair toward me just in time before I buckled.

Nina handed me a glass of water. "Unless you want something stronger, sugar?" Boy, I owed her one. Sloane had met his match with her.

I sipped at the water until I felt I could speak. "I apologize for what just happened. I don't know how he found out where I lived, but I am so sorry."

"Hush, now Dianne. Stop apologizing for the likes of that man. He's been put in his place and if he's smart that will be the last we see of him." Jan's gentle voice nearly brought me to tears.

"I can't thank all of you enough for banding together. I wish I could agree with you Jan, that Sloane has the intelligence to stay away." I finished my water, glad to see the tremors in my hands had stopped. "You've truly made me feel like family. And don't take this the wrong way, but I need to go for a drive. It's always therapeutic for me. I won't be gone long, promise!"

Alysha rubbed my shoulder. "I get it, Dianne. I'll run inside and get your purse and keys?"

"Thanks. I'm so sorry. This had been such a nice evening. Until he spoiled it. Jeff - let's have another barbecue soon?"

"Trust me, there'll be more. Are you sure you're okay though? Maybe someone should go with you?"

Before I could respond, Dax got my attention. "I was serious about laying assault charges, you know. But it's up to you."

I smiled. "I'll think about it if that's okay? And Jeff - thanks. I need to be alone for a bit. It's how I cope."

Both men nodded and backed away. The party broke up in earnest, and Alysha returned with my keys.

"Half an hour, I'll be back."

As I drove away, Jan's words came back to me. About hoping Sloane would be smart enough to never be seen around here again.

Her words would return to haunt me.

CHAPTER FIFTEEN
Alysha

I had no idea when Dianne returned home. She hadn't come back after about an hour. I was a little concerned, but Jeff and I decided to head into town for a couple of beers anyway. A reward for cleaning up after the barbecue. I knew how therapeutic a solo drive could be as well. And after the scene with Sloane, I'd bet she had a lot to think through.

The patio table we snagged provided a perfect view of the street. Not even mosquitoes were a deterrent to enjoying time spent with my guy on a summer's night. I enjoyed people watching, but Sloane Jackson better not be among them. We waved to some friends but neither of us was in the mood for darts or pool tonight. Besides, I needed to discuss a few things with Jeff. I let him enjoy one draft before I got serious.

"So, babe, is Leven Lodge giving you enough excitement?"

Not much of a response and I tried not to sigh in exasperation. "I've sure had enough for one day, but while we have some time to ourselves, I'd like to talk to you about my goals for my real estate business."

Jeff sipped at his beer but still said nothing. The vacant look on his face made me think he was miles away. My jaw clenched, and I tried to keep my voice even. "Babe - where are you? I've listened to you ad nauseum about the alpacas and the crias coming soon, a market stall, and your ambitions to expand the herd, so why can't you take *me* seriously about my aspirations? *Jeff!*"

He blinked twice and finally made eye contact with me. "Sorry babe. You're right - I get so wrapped up in all things alpaca I guess I *have* been neglecting you." He signaled the passing server for another round. "I know you want to get a career going, but can you manage it in addition to running the lodge?"

Not for the first time, I wondered how well he really knew me! "I may be little Jeff, but I'm young, healthy, and have lots of stamina. I'm so eager to get started, and it's what I want to do, but I'll need your help with the residents. If necessary, I'll bring someone part-time to help out."

His face clouded over. "Um, aren't you the one always concerned about too much overhead? An assistant doesn't come free, you know."

I'd have to give him a point on that score. "Yes, of course. Money is a concern, but the sooner I get started earning a commission, the sooner our cash flow improves."

I didn't want to argue with him. I was still feeling the stress from the altercation with Sloane, but it seemed we rarely had enough time to talk things through. Now I was the one sipping at my beer, playing for time.

"Have you thought this through enough, Aly? For example, what about start-up costs - where will that come from? You've already voiced your concerns about funds for my plans to increase the herd, right?"

The noise levels had increased. Saturdays tended to be boisterous, with strong music and loud conversation. Another couple settled at the table next to us. So, I waited a bit before I answered him. I recognized the lack of cash was going to be problematic for both our plans.

I needed to raise my voice to compensate for the growing din. "Financially, we can't add to the herd until we have permanent residents for the double room, and the room Nina has. Our profit margin is non-existent until then. As far as my start-up costs - minimal. I intend to get my foot in the door with a local agent. Get familiar with the area, that type of thing. That way between the commission and more rent coming, our income should increase. I plan to go over numbers with our accountant as well."

Jeff wasn't looking happy, and I tried to lighten the moment. "Oh, don't pout, my love. You have the new crias coming in a few weeks. That's exciting."

I only had to mention the baby alpacas and the smile returned to his face. "I'm not pouting. More like disappointed, I guess. And anxious to start on *my* plans."

I tilted my head to one side and lifted an eyebrow. He caught on and offered a sheepish grin. "And you're anxious to start on yours as well. Sorry. I can be an idiot sometimes."

"Only sometimes?" I teased him, but my heart was lighter.

"You advertised for the double room - any replies? At least we know people are looking at our new website."

Before I could answer, his brain raced back to his passion, and it wasn't me! "Oh, and Rick told me about a couple of male alpacas and a young female he said..."

My tender thoughts toward him vanished and I glared at him as he rattled on. I felt a headache growing, and the pub noise wasn't helping.

He must have picked up on my discomfort and reached for my hand. "Sorry, there I go again" His way to apologize or mollify me, was to ask me about my real estate plans. I wondered how much to share with him. He persisted. "Business is business, maybe I can pick up a few tips myself?"

I had no energy to nit-pick with him. "Once I've learned enough from a local broker, I'll go out on my own as an independent. Down the road, perhaps a small office in town, but to start I can work from the lodge. *A.Grant-Real Estate* or *Grant's Real Estate* are a couple of names I've thought of so far."

"Sounds good, babe. Do you have any connections yet?"

I laughed, but it sounded forced. "Matter of fact, yes. Dax says he knows a realtor and will introduce me."

"Your admirer has made his move, has he? Be careful Alysha, or I might get jealous. I know his type. Combined with the authority of a police officer, could spell trouble."

Oh, for Pete's sake. Could he give it a rest already? "Trust me, there is nothing to be jealous of. If he wasn't Jan's nephew, I'd brush him off, but I can handle him."

"*Grant's Real Estate*, eh?" His eyes twinkled. "I should get my act together and marry you, so we can call it *Iverson Real Estate*."

We had only hinted at getting married, so this was as close to a proposal as I'd probably get. I should have been happy, but instead, I was irritated at his assumption.

"I think that's the beer talking, and besides who says I'd change my name to Iverson?"

And then I felt guilty. What I'd said was hurtful and I tried to downplay it. "Let's get our lives sorted out first before we start down the aisle. Whether we're married or not, this is a partnership, right? So, I promise I'll help you with your herd increase plans if you do the same for me. I see the potential in Grant's Crossing for all kinds of expansion. The new spa and restaurant will bring lots of potential buyers from the city."

Jeff lifted his pint of beer and clinked my glass. "Cheers, Aly. I'm so proud of you and I'll help, I promise. Here's to Grant's or Iverson Real Estate."

As we finished the last of our beers, a familiar person reached our table. I wasn't unhappy that we were getting ready to leave.

"Hi, you two. Did I miss anything tonight at the lodge? How was the barbecue?"

I smiled at Cassie. No way would I tell her about the Sloane incident. It would spread around the pub like wildfire. "Our resident barbecue king, in your absence, did a fine job. Satisfied customers all around. You can hear all about it on Monday. But for now, we're calling it a night."

***

Late Sunday afternoon brought more unsettled weather - the rolling heavy clouds promised a thunderstorm. Not enough to keep the diehards from sitting out on the veranda, though, while Nina entertained them with a story.

She'd spent most of the day secluded in her room, hatching devious plots for her new book, no doubt. So maybe she was enjoying the break from writing a little too much. I had to give her credit; she was a born storyteller. And while I wasn't sure if she spoke truth or fiction, both Minnie and Philip were enraptured listeners. High praise for Nina as those two rarely pay attention to what anyone ever has to say.

It must have been an interesting story as Dianne was also listening attentively to Nina. Perhaps after the debacle with Sloane Jackson yesterday they would be friends or at least allies. Stranger things have happened. I walked away from the house, down the main driveway, and looked back at the Lodge.

I viewed the old farmhouse with fresh eyes, admiring its architecture and how the renovations had stayed true to its original build. Maybe my love of real estate had been fostered at an early age by this home. Not for the first time, I thanked my lucky stars to have this wonderful place as my home.

I headed back toward the house and wandered around the side. There was Jan, tending to what she loves, her herb and vegetable gardens. I waved my hand in greeting and was about to speak when I heard an approaching vehicle.

Now what?

Jan straightened, laid aside her trowel, and removed her gardening gloves. I moved closer to her, and she pointed to the unmarked police car. She smiled, and uttered, "He can't stay away from you."

I groaned inwardly as she continued. "It's Dax and young Dubois. Perhaps with more information on poor Andrew. An arrest?"

Dax and his partner, Steven Dubois had left the car and moved toward us. I stood rooted to the ground and my inward groan strengthened as they brought their serious and unsmiling faces forward to stop in front of us.

Dax was all business and barely acknowledged his aunt. "Good afternoon Ms. Grant. We're sorry to disturb everyone but we're here on official business. We'd like a word with Dianne Mitchell."

I spun my head toward the veranda, where the storytelling had stopped. All heads now stared in my direction. They were too far away to hear Dax's request, but I could see Minnie muttering. And Lily's mouth was a big round O. Rose had moved next to her, ready to be the consoling sister.

"Dianne? Official business for what? Dax, is this really necessary?" Part of me found it odd Jan hadn't said a word, as if she was leaving this all up to me. Our peaceful Sunday afternoon had vanished.

"The residents aren't going to be happy you've interrupted their siesta time." I tried to make light of the request, but Dax was beyond small talk. I made eye contact with Dianne and crooked my finger at her to join us. She averted her eyes and ignored me.

At the same time, Jeff rounded the house. He'd yet to recognize the sombre mood and was all smiles. "Hey, Dax. How ya doing? Back for more of my cooking?"

Dax brushed Jeff off with a curt nod and headed toward the veranda. His heavy black boots thudded on the wooden steps, and he kept one hand tucked into his gun belt. I nearly had to run to keep up with him. All eyes watched as Dax zeroed in on Dianne. To all appearances, she was unperturbed - relaxing in a comfortable basket chair. But I saw the tic under her eye as Dax came closer to her.

"Ms. Mitchell, we'd like you to come with us to the station to answer a few questions and assist in an ongoing inquiry."

Her voice was eerily calm. "About what?"

"I'd prefer not to speak in front of the others."

"I see. Well, Detective, I'm always happy to help the police. Shall we?"

And without a look back at us, the three of them headed to the police cruiser.

I called after them, unsure of what exactly to say, but sounding completely useless when I said. "Keep us posted, Dianne. If you need a ride back home..."

Dax opened his door and addressed Jan and me. "It may be a few hours. If not before, then you'll hear about the news with tomorrow's Gazette."

And then they were gone, leaving us all stunned.

CHAPTER SIXTEEN
Dianne

My chauffeur wasn't forthcoming about the nature of our trip into town. And Dax wouldn't say butter if his mouth was full of it. At least this was a new experience. Riding in the back of a police car. The fact neither officer was speaking to me caused a twinge of anxiety. But I knew I hadn't done anything wrong, so assumed they needed me to assist with an investigation. Then I spied Mrs. Friedman, strolling along the sidewalk, facing my direction, and I sank lower in the seat. The proverbial town gossip. If she saw me, then for sure I'd be guilty of something.

I sat up straight when we parked in front of the police station. Well, when I say police station, I mean a storefront location not much bigger than a convenience store. I guess it could be called a substation, and I doubt it contained more than one cell. Dax opened my door and I followed him inside. He still hadn't spoken to me.

We went straight to a small room. No window and atrocious overhead lighting! The walls could use a fresh coat of hospital green as well. If I were a criminal, I'd confess just to get out of there.

The table we sat at took up most of the room. They offered me water which I accepted. But it was like waiting for the other shoe to drop. What on earth did they want with me?

Typical me. I hate dead air. "So, gentlemen, how can I help you today?"

Dax cleared his throat and opened a small black notebook. I wondered if all police forces shopped at the same stationery store. "We'd like to ask you about your activities yesterday."

"My *activities*? Can you be a little more specific? You were at the barbecue with me, so you already know that."

"Let's start with the barbecue then. At approximately 6:30 p.m. a man identified as Sloane Jackson arrived. He hadn't been invited, is that correct?"

Sloane! Would I never be free of the hold he had on my life? "Trust me, I didn't invite him. Not likely anyone else at the lodge did either. Classic Sloane move to insert himself into a place he's not wanted."

"So, you admit you have a history with Mr. Sloane?"

Tiny alarm bells started ringing. What had he done now? I'd seen enough cop shows to know how easy it was to implicate yourself without trying. And without knowing the nature of their questions, I thought I'd better be careful. I wouldn't put it past Sloane to have a trumped-up charge brought against me!

"Yes, I do."

I caught a smile on Dubois' face, but he suppressed it almost as fast as Dax fired more questions at me. "Can you elaborate, please? What kind of relationship do you, or did you, have? For how long?"

Was Dax going to charge Sloane with assault, and if so, was I ready for what that might entail? I preferred to let the past be in the past. And then I recalled the vehemence in Nina's voice when she called him for what he was. Would I be selfish to not lay a charge - especially if it prevented him from abusing someone else?

"Right, then Dax. I mean DC Young. I'll lay a charge against Sloane Jackson for assault. What do I need to tell you?"

Dubois threw Dax a puzzled look, who also looked confused. What had I missed?

Dax recovered first. "We'll get to that later, Ms. Mitchell. Let's get back to my question. Your relationship with Jackson. How long did it last?"

I chose my words carefully. "I met Sloane about five years ago when I worked in Toronto. We briefly dated, but I didn't care for the jealous and abusive turn the relationship took and ended it." They didn't comment, so I carried on. "As you may have determined, DC Young, Sloane is not one to take no for an answer. He wouldn't accept what I wanted out of our relationship, such as it was and began to harass me. It was the excuse I needed to retire - truthfully, I quit - and move away from Toronto. I came here about four years ago. Saw him in town earlier on Friday, but until then I'd had no contact with him, and no desire to do so, either."

I finished speaking and realized my hands were clenched in my lap. I forced them to relax while I watched Dax scribble more notes.

"And after the barbecue, you went for a drive, correct? Where did your drive take you and did anyone see you?"

Okay, this question didn't fit with my assumption about laying a charge against Sloane. I tried to make light of the question. "Is this where I ask to see my lawyer?"

Dax leaned across the table. "Do you need a lawyer?" Without a hint of joking in his voice my stomach flip-flopped. What was going on?

I thought carefully before I answered. "I drove around for a couple of hours. Nowhere specific and didn't stop anywhere. I do it a lot, ask Jan. It helps me calm down."

"Calm down from what?" Dubois' question seemed obvious.

"Dax, tell him what Sloane said at the barbecue. You saw how upset I was!"

"Upset enough to utter a death threat." He checked his notebook. *'I could just kill you for what you did to me.'*

"What!" Oh my God, you had to be kidding me. This was getting ridiculous.

Dubois had more. "And you uttered a threat earlier, at the Crossings Tavern. I quote, *'If you died tomorrow, I wouldn't shed a tear'* and *'You can go to hell for all I care. More than one body's been found in that river. I'd be careful.'* People and their cell phones - useful at times."

I sputtered, "But everyone says things like that when they're upset or feel threatened. I wouldn't actually kill him." My mouth had gone dry, and I kept licking my lips.

Without responding to what I'd said, Dubois cut to the chase. "Sloane Jackson was found murdered outside the home he was renting on River Drive. Time of death is estimated between 9:00 p.m. and midnight Saturday."

And that's when I fainted.

CHAPTER SEVENTEEN
Alysha

I enjoyed reading the newspaper in the morning with my first cup of coffee, but not today. Of course, I was dismayed to read of yet another murder in Grant's Crossing. The paper noted an unidentified man was found in a rental property on River Road. All signs of blunt force trauma. Police once more are investigating. I felt bad thinking ill of the dead, but I found it difficult to be sorry that odious Sloane Jackson was dead. Dianne didn't return from her police questioning until after midnight and then needed to speak with Jan and me. We were beyond shocked that she was under suspicion of his murder and debated whether she should be contacting a lawyer. Or would that be seen as a sure sign of guilt?

My head was spinning. A run with Jeff this morning was needed to clear my mind. I was dressed and ready, but he was taking his time. Dwelling on Dianne being suspected of murder, and the newspaper article fed into my growing irritation. Too much around me seemed out of my control.

"Jeff! We're running this morning, remember?"

He emerged from the bathroom. "Yes, I remember and it's a good idea, but you're not too tired? You tossed and turned all night."

I lowered my impatience level. "I'll be fine. And I'm sorry if I snapped at you. Too much on my mind. So, are you ready to run?"

"Just about. I need to talk to Frank about one little thing first, okay?"

"Sure. Talk to him and I'll meet you in the driveway. Ten minutes, right?"

I made my way downstairs and managed to avoid everyone. They'd all be eager for details about Dianne, but I wasn't in the mood. I heard the vacuum running, so Jan was already busy with her chores.

I did a few stretches but was itching to get going. I did my best thinking when running and there was a lot on my mind. *Let's go, Jeff.*

At last. That was long ten minutes, but I didn't comment. My partner and best friend tapped his ball cap and said "We're off. Which direction, babe."

"I don't care. Let's see if we can get in a few clicks then head for the coffee shop."

"Sounds like a plan. Maybe you can let me in as to what happened at the police station with Dianne last night. You didn't want to talk about it after she got home."

We set off down the driveway and ran side by side. One of my favourite things to do.

"Thanks for being patient with me. I was feeling overwhelmed but let's wait until we stop before we get into the foibles of living at Leven Lodge."

He turned and smiled at me. "Okay, let's pick up the pace a little. I'll race you to the bridge and the loser buys coffee. Deal?"

"You're on!"

Half an hour later my legs started to burn. Which slowed me down and resulted in me buying the coffee at the Java Hut. Jeff crowed how much fitter he was than me. Not the best way to get on my good side today.

"I guess I'm more tired than I thought." We sat in a booth sharing quiet time and we discussed the unlikely idea that Dianne could have anything to do with Sloane Jackson's death.

The main street was busy for a Monday and there were plenty of early-morning shoppers. The sky threatened rain, so we decided to head back and avoid getting caught in a downpour.

Jeff reached for my hand across the table. "It's going to be alright, Alysha. We all heard what she said to that character. Dax included. But we all say things when we're angry. Even Nina had a few choice words to send him on his way. The police will find out who did it. By all accounts, he was no saint."

"That's neither here nor there, Jeff. We don't know anything about him except he's an investor in the Rivermill location. The police will get results." I downed the rest of my coffee. "And I know it sounds bad, selfish, when I say, another murder in town does not fit well with my real estate ambitions. How can we expect to attract customers to our bucolic town when people are getting murdered?"

"Alysha! It's not like you to be so negative." He gathered up our empty cups for the trash and conveniently changed the subject. "For now, let's get home before we get caught in the storm. Maybe you can offer support to Dianne. Sitting under a cloud of suspicion can't be very comfortable."

I decided not to reply. We left the coffee shop and hit the pavement. We were halfway home before the rain came down in buckets. It wasn't cold but we resembled drowned rats. We kept going, with the lodge in our sightlines.

"Whoa! I don't like the look of this, Aly." Jeff slowed to a walk and pointed to the scene we were approaching.

Parked behind Dax's police car was a flatbed tow truck. I could see Jan on the top step of the veranda, speaking with him. Even at a distance her rigid stance portended bad news. Dubois stood next to the car. Neither in detective suits today, but in uniform. Drawing closer I saw Dax held a folded piece of paper in his hand.

Normally we'd have entered at the side of the house, but we joined them on the veranda. This was no social visit. Jan tense and Dax in full-blown official police mode.

He turned to greet me with a curt nod, "Ms. Grant." He held the paper close enough for me to see it was a search warrant. My heart skipped a beat, and not in a good way. "We need the keys to Dianne Mitchell's car. Part of the investigation."

"You can't seriously believe she had anything to do with Jackson's murder? Dax?" My hands trembled, whether from fear or indignation I couldn't tell.

"It's not for me to comment." He turned to look at his aunt. "I would prefer Ms. Mitchell give us the keys, but I can go inside and ask her myself?"

Great, I supposed that was his way of trying to be understanding. Well, he wasn't coming inside my house. "I'll go and talk to her. You stay here - officer."

***

I couldn't figure Dax out. Talk about mixed messages. He's either flirting with me or all business. I understood being here on police matters, but seriously! I put the thought on hold till later. Right now, I was more concerned for Dianne.

I took the stairs two at a time to reach Dianne's room. My shoes squelched on the steps. Water continued to drip from my curls, and I longed to dry off. Damn Dax anyway.

"Dianne?" I tapped on her door, and she opened it. Her eyes widened at my soaking wet self.

"Out of towels this morning? I'll grab one. C'mon in."

I followed her into the room, which was dark. No lights turned on even though it was a dreary day.

"I'll take the towel, thanks. But that's not why I'm here. Dianne, I need your car keys."

She stopped in her tracks. "My car keys? Sure, but why? Is that why you're soaked - did your car break down?"

The towel was soon forgotten as I told her about the search warrant for her car.

She slumped into her chair by the window. "I knew it. I haven't slept all night. Waiting for the other shoe to drop, and now it has."

I waffled. I wanted to comfort her but knew Dax stood downstairs eager for her keys. I certainly didn't want him coming up here and seeing her in a funk.

"Is that why you're sitting in the dark? Sorry, Dianne, I don't mean to sound abrupt, but I don't want the police coming up here and seeing you in this state."

She nodded and leaned down to her handbag by her feet. After a moment of rummaging, she held up the key. "Take it." Her tone was listless.

I think I was more concerned seeing her bummed out than what the police would be doing with her car. I hugged her, unable to imagine what was going through her head. Reluctantly, I left her sitting by the window— in the dark. Making my way downstairs I mentally reviewed the little I knew about what the police had on Jackson's death. Not for a second did I believe she'd killed him. All circumstantial, or she would have been arrested. I re-joined Jeff and Jan on the veranda and handed the keys to Dax.

"Can I give Dianne an idea when she'll have her car back?"

"Sorry, it's not up to me. It will depend on what turns up in the search."

How could he be so cold! My voice rose an octave. "Search? Search for what? A murder weapon, fingerprints? What? She didn't do it!"

Jeff stood closer to me. He intervened before my motor mouth did damage, or, more likely before I embarrassed him. "Alysha, I'm sure it's all part of normal police procedures. Dax has to do his job."

I glared at him as I pushed him away. Guys sticking together. Would have been nice if he'd backed me up. I fumed inside. I looked at Jan and mouthed *later*. She nodded, so I knew she got the message that we should talk. At least *she's* on my side. I turned on my heel, ignoring the clueless look on Jeff's face, and escaped to the sanctuary of our apartment.

CHAPTER EIGHTEEN
Dianne

Alysha left, and I ran down the hall to the McTaggart's old room. I stepped out on the room's balcony just in time to see my car pulled onto a flatbed truck. My hands gripped the railing and tears threatened. I hadn't done anything wrong, but how could I prove it? Dax looked up; his face expressionless.

"Fine mess you're in now. Gonna get a lawyer?"

I jumped when Minnie spoke. She'd crept up behind me ninja-style, her bulging knitting bag drooping from one arm. I was ready with a sharp response but stopped when I saw concern in her eyes. An off day for her.

"No need for a lawyer, Minnie, but thanks for asking."

She clucked, turned, and was gone with no further comment.

I didn't know what to do with myself. It would be awkward to go downstairs, and now I had no wheels to escape with either. Didn't feel like talking to Alysha or Jan. My room would have to do for now.

Down the hallway scrabbling nails on the floor caught my attention. Hemingway pranced at the end of a glittery leash wrapped around Nina's hand.

"Dianne. We're heading out for a walk."

Well thanks, Captain Obvious. "I see that. Have fun." Was I supposed to have a witty retort to her revelation?

"Helps clear the cobwebs for me as well as a potty break for snookums." She hesitated before taking another step. "Observation permitted, sunshine? Looks like you could do with some fresh air, too. Come with us."

What the heck, why not? But I'd contain my enthusiasm. "Best offer I've had today, thanks."

She didn't pursue the remark and we headed down the stairs. Luck was with me, and no one saw us leave by the back door. We strolled toward the barn area, stopping every couple of feet for Hemingway to do his dog thing. I should have changed my shoes. The heavy grass, which needed cutting, was sopping wet.

"Out with it. How are you doing, chickie?"

Crap, if another person voiced concern for me, I'd lose it. "I've had better days, that's for sure."

She fussed with her scarf. "For what it's worth, I'm well acquainted with low-life vermin like Mr. Jackson. I've had to put more than one cretin like him in his place. Take it from me, someone's done the world a favour."

"So, you don't think I had anything to do with it?"

She reached to the ground, small baggie in hand, and cleaned up the doggy-doo. "What a good boy!" In response the creature stood on hind legs, begging to have those paws removed from the offending grass. A quick wipe of tiny wet feet and Hemingway was once again swaddled within Nina's scarf. Then she turned her attention to me.

"No, I don't. I don't see you as a stupid person."

Gotta love back-handed compliments. "Thanks, I think."

We sat on a nearby bench. The alpacas were off in the distance grazing. I almost envied them. Might be nice to have a mindless occupation like that for a change.

She smirked. "But cops! Once they peg you as guilty, it won't matter what you say."

"Exactly. It's why I think I should get a lawyer, but if I do then they'll think it's a show of guilt. Catch-22."

"Listen, chickie. Take it from one who knows. Stand your ground. You did nothing wrong so prove it, or at least act like it. Get a lawyer. Innocent people get railroaded all the time."

"You might be right."

"Do you have a lawyer?"

"Not exactly. There's old Lockhart in town, but I think he only does real estate and wills. He might be able to refer me to someone."

"Good. And if not, I have the name of a good criminal lawyer in Toronto. He's also become a *friend*, of sorts, and if I asked, I know he'd drive up here for you."

Despite my worry about the police and Sloane, I was curious about Nina's connection to a criminal lawyer. "Sounds like you've had some experience?"

She threw her head back and laughed out loud. "Oh, yes, I've had experience. And you know what they say about writers. Write what you know!"

I turned her comment into a change of subject. "And you're still wanting to write about what happened to us here last year?"

She fussed over the dog for a minute before replying. "Between you and me, sunshine, I may have changed my mind."

What? I waited for her to go on.

"Thing is, when I started on this project, you were all strangers to me. I've never written about real people before." She tapped the side of her head. "I prefer to create my characters from scratch. But now I've come to know some of you, and it's changed my perspective. I like Alysha. She's got spunk. As do you!"

I didn't feel so spunky at the moment, but I'd buy what she was selling. "What are you going to do?"

She chuckled. "Won't be the first time I've re-written a work in progress. Although, that Minnie. I'd sure like to know her back story."

"Wouldn't we all. Or maybe not."

We shared a laugh, and I realized my spirits had lifted. And I surprised myself to find I liked Nina. Which led to my suggestion. "If not Minnie, I'd bet there's a story around the twins' childhood. Am I wrong?"

"You have a writer's imagination, Dianne. I've never met anyone who didn't have a story to tell."

Oh, yes and I'm sure she had a story as well. Once my life settled back to boring and routine, I hoped she'd share, with me at least, before her stay at the lodge was done.

The sun had finally broken through the clouds, and I knew my gloomy slump was over. "Thanks for the pep talk. I might even be able to face the crew at dinner this evening."

"Never let 'em know what's bugging you, that's what I say."

"Agreed." I turned my attention back to the house. Jeff was lugging boxes and bags from the inside and loading his pick-up. "Ah. It would appear Minnie has released more treasures out into the world. She's been hoarding stuff for years, and have you seen her pocket food after meals?"

Nina wrinkled her nose. "And no one says anything to her about it? I can't believe she eats everything she takes. She's as thin as a rake."

"I know. Must be the nervous energy burns off any calories. Jan tolerated a lot of her behaviour, but after Alysha arrived last year, things have slowly changed. I've been sharing a bathroom with Minnie since I've been here, and sometimes the air currents from under the door have been downright gag worthy. So, I'd bet the pilfered food doesn't get eaten."

"And is there a story between her and Frank?"

Nina the writer was back, and I didn't feel inclined to offer up theories. "Good question." I hoped that was non-committal enough for her.

I rose from the bench. "The sun feels so good after too many days of rain. I'd go for a drive if I had my car."

Nina tilted her head to one side. "I've got mine. So, here's a suggestion. Let's both avoid the dinner meal this evening and head into town. I heard someone mention a legion. Lots of stories there. Maybe some new inspiration."

"Why not. Sure. We need to let Jan know, so she has a proper head count for meal planning. What time were you thinking?"

We started our walk back to the house. "How about later this afternoon. About four-thirty. Maybe you can give me a guided tour of the town?"

I eyed the beady black eyes peeking out from under her scarf. "What about Hemingway?"

"He'll be fine on his own for a few hours. Won't you, snuggums?"

Just when I was feeling mellow toward her, she had to go and fawn all over the mutt again. Ugh! If my eyes rolled any further back in my head, I could see where I was coming from.

"Right. Okay, I'll go find Jan and let her know we won't be here for dinner. See you later, Nina."

She offered a distracted wave as she released Hemingway down onto the grass. I gave my head a shake and went inside looking for Jan.

"Jan - are you here?"

"Laundry."

She leaned over the dryer, punched the settings, and turned around to give me her motherly eye. "How are you doing, Dianne?"

I shrugged. "I guess it could be worse."

"You know Dax is only doing his job? He may have his faults, but I think he felt pretty uncomfortable taking your car away."

"It's okay. Believe it or not, Nina and I have been talking and she managed to cheer me up."

"Hmmm. If you say so."

"And I came to tell you, she and I will be heading into town for supper, so don't set a place for us."

"The heads-up is always appreciated, and I'll let Cassie know. It'll do you good to have a break from here for a few hours."

"Yep, my feelings, too. See you later."

My thoughts turned to what I could wear, when a crash from the second floor made us both jump.

CHAPTER NINETEEN
Alysha

I collided with Jan and Dianne on the second floor. "Guess you heard it too? Where did it come from?"

We looked at each other and came to the same conclusion. Minnie.

Jan knocked on her door. "Minnie are you all right in there? Did something fall over?" We heard scuffling from the room and the sounds of crying.

"Minnie, it's Alysha. Please open the door."

"No, no. Go away."

"I insist Minnie. If you won't open it, I will. We're worried about you."

"Who's *we*? Those busybodies who want to know everything about my business. Why can't you leave me alone? I'm fine."

The crying we heard from the other side of the door indicated otherwise. Jan nodded at me and handed over the keys; I put my hand on the door handle and turned to Dianne.

"Could you please find Frank? He's working with Jeff in the barn. He has a way of dealing with her, which seems to calm her down."

"Of course."

She began to run down the stairs, as Jan and I entered Minnie's room. Our mouths gaped with shock at the sight. If we thought Minnie was always in a disheveled state before, how she looked now was nothing short of... I couldn't find the words.

I wondered if the tidying up of her room had moved some furniture in a negative way. Furniture that may have been piled up but had been a support of sorts to other pieces.

Because now a floor-to-ceiling bookcase had toppled, and its contents were strewn everywhere. It had crashed onto the wooden cradle sitting under the window, smashing it to pieces. Minnie sat on the floor holding parts of the broken cradle, disconsolate, and sobbing as if her heart would break.

Jan reached her first. "Oh, Minnie. Are you hurt? And your lovely cradle. Perhaps it can be fixed. Let me help you."

She didn't answer but kept crying while she held on to a broken part of the cradle. I was frozen to the spot and inwardly berated myself for feeling useless.

Jan's gentle, but in-charge voice got through to me. "Alysha, can you help me get her up? We can sit her on the bed if you take one arm?"

I no longer saw an unlikeable old woman, but a wounded soul. I had a feeling she wasn't physically hurt but had a sorrow we wouldn't be able to comfort. I gently took her other arm and helped Jan bring her to her feet. We led her to sit on the edge of her bed. She still clutched a piece of the shattered cradle.

Jan spoke softly to her and stroked her arm. "Can we put this aside for a minute? I'd like to make sure you're not hurt anywhere."

Minnie let out a wail and held tighter to the broken piece of wood. Through her sobs, she choked out, "It's all I have left, it's all I have left."

I looked at Jan. "What can we do for her?" But before she could answer, Frank arrived, with Dianne right behind. The concern on his face confirmed he would be the one to handle her right now.

He sat beside her on the bed. "Minnie, love? Hush now, it will be alright."

She paused her sobbing and turned to look at him as if only just aware he'd arrived. "Frank? It's broken, destroyed!"

I watched in amazement as he put his arm around her and pulled her head to his shoulder. He looked up at us and whispered. "Can I ask you all to leave the room, please? She needs some space. I'll talk to her and see what's going on here."

I willingly let Jan take control of the situation, as she ushered Dianne and me from the room.

We moved into the hallway, out of hearing range. Always the voice of reason, Jan had the right suggestion. "Let's leave her with Frank and I'll make us some coffee."

As we walked down the stairs, Jan continued. "I'm not sure what that's all about. I've never seen her so upset, but I'm grateful Frank seems to know what to do."

Dianne had finally found her voice. "Clearly, the cradle holds special meaning, and I'd bet Frank knows something about it."

I shouldn't have been surprised that Dianne's inquisitive side had come to the surface. What did surprise me was feeling protective towards Minnie! "If he wants to share, I'm sure he will. And unless she's physically hurt, it's not for us to pry."

"I agree, little one. Let's wait and see, shall we?" Having Jan on side with me, made me feel better.

An hour later, we finally heard Frank's footsteps on the stairs. He made his way to the kitchen, where he looked at each of us in turn and nodded.

"She's calm for now, and she wasn't hurt, but some decisions need to be made. I suppose you want an explanation?"

I looked to Dianne and Jan for some input, but it appeared I was back in charge. "Only if you want to share, Frank. Does she need a doctor?"

Jan stood, put a finger to her lips, and suggested we go to her sitting room for some privacy.

Once settled, the floor was Frank's. He paced and rubbed one hand through his thinning hair. He looked uncomfortable, as if unsure of how to proceed.

"Frank, sit, please. You'll wear a hole in my carpet." Jan's admonition to her guest was tempered with concern.

He halted, turned, and smiled. Then lowered himself into the nearest chair. "Sorry, ladies. Trying to put my thoughts in order. And I know you must have questions. Lots of questions."

Dianne and I nodded but didn't interrupt him.

"Minnie's permitted me to share what I know with you. She has reservations, of course, but it's time she was better understood."

We sat on the edge of our seats; Dianne and Jan were still drinking coffee. If I had any more, I'd be jumping out of my skin. Jan looked at me, so I prompted him. "Take your time, Frank. We're all worried about Minnie, never having seen that side of her. Something traumatic triggered her behaviour."

Dianne placed her coffee cup on the table and turned to Frank. "Would you prefer I leave? Maybe this should be just you three?"

"No Dianne, you live here with Minnie and need to hear this too." Frank cleared his throat and began. "Contrary to how Minnie is now, you might not believe how lovely she was as a young woman." He paused, drew in a deep breath, then slowly released it. "Jan, you may have known Minnie since she moved in here almost twenty years ago but, I fell for her hard, many years before that, and we had plans to marry. She became pregnant - and you can imagine the shame our families put on us back then - but we were so happy planning our life together."

He paused and closed his eyes for a moment. I knew what memories could do. Take you on a trip you might not be prepared for. We gave him his space and then he continued. "It was not to be. At six months - before we could marry - she miscarried, and all our dreams were shattered. It was not just the melancholy of losing the baby... something snapped inside her, and she eventually became the woman you see today. She moved away from Grant's Crossing for a long time, and I didn't see her until she returned."

Dianne had leaned so far forward in her chair, she was in danger of slipping to the floor. *Curiosity killed the cat* popped into my mind.

"Where did she disappear to? Why didn't you get married when she returned? I bet you made the cradle, right?"

"Dianne! Give the man a chance to finish." Jan's tone put the brakes on any more questions.

"It's okay, Jan. Yes, Dianne, I made the cradle which is now in pieces. And to answer your other questions. Well, Minnie's parents thought it best she was hospitalized for a while. And as to why we were never married? Turns out, it wasn't meant to be. Minnie pushed everyone away, including me. But I've always managed to stay close by."

"That's to your credit, Frank. Not many would have." Jan's eyes glistened and I had to wipe away a tear, too. "Can I get you a drink of water, or something stronger?"

"A glass of water would be good, Jan, thank you."

We waited in silence until she returned with a glass for him, and then Dianne - like a dog with a bone - attacked again. "So, what happened then, after she returned?"

"She managed to find a retail job in town. I'd see her from time to time, usually at a distance, and then a few years later, she needed an operation. Woman stuff."

I tried not to smile. Older men, and some young ones, still felt awkward with any mention of female issues.

"And that's when Estelle took her in here to convalesce. As I'd worked for the Grants for many years, I was delighted to still be near her."

Jan hadn't uttered a word, and now Dianne had tears in her eyes. Time to bring the past up to date before we ran out of tissue. "Thank you, Frank. You've shed a whole different light on her, and I think we can all agree we need to do what's best for her in whatever way we can. Do you think she should see a doctor, or benefit from therapy?"

"I'm no medical person, Alysha, so I don't know. Probably wouldn't hurt to have her see a doctor. Goodness knows when she last had a check-up. Jan?"

"I have no idea, Frank. But I suspect the answer would be never. I agree it would be a good thing. There should be a contact name on her file, and I'll make a call."

Frank nodded. "I feel a burden has been lifted, from me, at least. She never wanted to share any of this, but today's events have changed everything. Who knows? I thought I noticed a change in her the last few months. Coincidentally, since you arrived, Alysha."

"Really? Wow, I don't know what to say, except I hope it's a good change!" Frank's comment had taken me completely by surprise.

He carried on. "I have a feeling being faced with a room clean-up is going to help immensely. Oh, and I've just thought of something else she admitted to me. The food you found in there? She'd been saving it for when the baby was hungry."

My hand flew to my mouth. "Aw, that is so sad. But I think it does indicate she needs help more than we can provide."

"You're probably right. We'll find her the best we can. And perhaps with encouragement from me, and all of you, as friends, it will be just the ticket to turn things around for her."

Jan looked thoughtful. "Perhaps she'd let one of the healers from the reserve talk with her? What do you think, or would she object?"

Frank laughed, "Object? Of course, she will. Doesn't she always, but I'll discuss it with her and let you know. Dianne, you have another question, I can tell."

We all chuckled, and the mood lightened.

"C'mon, Frank. We all need to know. What about the knitting?"

"Ah yes. It does seem to go hand in hand with her, doesn't it? No surprise when she found out she was pregnant she started making baby clothes. Her hands flew with those needles. Not sure whatever happened to the clothes she made." His gaze grew unfocused for a moment, then he shook his head. "Come to think of it, I always saw her knitting, but hardly ever saw a hat or mittens, or anything for a baby -

especially after the miscarriage. She's still knitting like a fiend, and I've never seen a blessed thing."

Jan smiled. "It makes some sense now. I've seen her knitting over the years, and then I've seen her pick the yarn apart, unraveling whatever she'd made. Repeatedly. Perhaps a visible expression of how her mind was behaving at times? The mind can work in mysterious ways."

Jan's wisdom continued to impress me, and what she said sounded logical. I didn't know about the others, but I felt drained. She kept an optimistic tone. "Let's all rally around her and offer support. With any luck, some of her other habits might ease off, too?"

Dianne snorted. "Well, there goes my fun at mealtimes - just kidding."

I'd bet she didn't mean to say that out loud! I stood. "Count on you, Dianne, to have a different *viewpoint*."

"I was only kidding, honest!"

Time to change the subject, so I turned to Frank. "We'll have her see a doctor, but in the meantime, what can we do for her right now? Should we let her rest? Pretend nothing's happened?"

Everyone was standing now, and Frank answered. "Might be best to not draw attention to what's happened, especially with the others, you know? I'll have Jeff help me clear the rest of her room so it's habitable by the end of the day. Let's look at today as the first steps on the road to recovery for her. Your support and understanding will mean a lot, even if she doesn't know how to thank you."

"Of course, please do what you can for her, and I can only speak for myself, but I'll put in a better effort to be more understanding." I looked at Jan and Dianne and received nods of agreement.

"I'll be off then. You ladies take care."

Frank left us - the three amigos - standing in comforting silence until Jan spoke. "Another crisis averted. I have work to do and start dinner preparations. Are you not going into town, Dianne, with Nina? Why don't you join them, Alysha?"

The suggestion was followed by a warning. "And I don't have to tell either of you I'll have your heads if there is even a hint disclosed around what has been discussed this afternoon."

I recognized a dismissal when I heard one and didn't have to be told twice. I knew I'd never breach the confidences spoken here today, but Dianne?

CHAPTER TWENTY
Dianne

As I dressed for my evening out with Nina, I reflected on what had just happened. Wonders would never cease. Our Minnie is human after all. I'd have to make the effort, like Alysha, to be kinder in the future. Who hasn't had something in their past with the potential to mess you up? I was living proof. A diversion this evening wasn't a bad thing, and I anticipated a lively couple of hours with Nina.

She'd probably want to talk, so a quieter venue than the Crossings Tavern, or legion, would be a better choice. And seeing as Alysha had declined to join us, I thought *Katie's Kitchen* would work. Good menu, no pressure to hurry through a meal, and decent wine selection. Read between the lines - suited for a mature clientele who prefer not to shout at their dinner companions to be heard.

She'd have to drive so I could be less responsible with my wine intake. And I briefly wondered if the damn dog would be coming with us. Part of me wanted to stay back and be at the table for dinner to see what was said about Minnie. Anyone in their rooms earlier would have heard the commotion.

A knock at my door pushed any more thoughts away. "Dianne? It's a little after four - you said you wanted to leave about now?"

"Be right there, Nina."

Tucking my purse under my arm I opened the door. Oh, so glad I decided against wearing anything yellow. Here we go again. Nina sported fluorescent yellow capris, with a yellow and white striped tunic top. My eyes were drawn to her white sandals, decorated with tiny sunflowers. I'd need my sunglasses well after sunset! She dangled her car keys. "I'll drive."

"Perfect, and I'll pick the location if that's okay?" I was relieved to see no sign of her muse.

"Your town, chickie. Let's go."

I heard Jan in the dining room and poked my head in. "We're off, Jan. Probably going to *Katie's*."

She shooed me with her apron. "Enjoy, and don't hurry back."

***

I wondered how many tickets Nina had racked up over the years as we sped into town. Dax and crew were missing out on guaranteed income while she stayed here. But I suppose a murder investigation takes priority. Lucky break for Nina!

We didn't talk much on the drive, although I pointed out a few places of interest along the way. "There's *Books and More*. You might want to check that out while you're here. Oh, and the bakery! The best eclairs ever - but don't tell Cassie!"

I indicated the turn she needed, and we arrived at Katie's Kitchen. Mondays wouldn't be too busy, so I opted for a booth in the back when the server seated us.

Menus were handed out and Nina enquired about a bottle of wine. "Red okay with you?" she asked.

I recognized the label and only hoped that because she chose it, she'd be paying for it! "Sounds good."

I'd ordered the grilled salmon and a salad, while Nina settled on a steak. We made small talk about books and life in a small town until the food arrived. I realized that between hearing about Minnie and thinking about this evening, I'd put the cloud of suspicion hanging over my head far away.

Until Nina reminded me. "Have you heard any more from the police?"

"Nothing yet. I suppose no news is good news."

"Or it's a tactic to unnerve you." She winked as she stabbed another fry on her plate.

"Sounds like you'd know a thing or two about that?"

She tossed her back head and gave a throaty laugh. "Sugar, let's just say I've had some life experiences." Then she grew serious. "I don't mean to make light of your situation, sorry. But I'd like to help if I can."

I considered her offer. "Not sure how you can help but, I'll let you know. I tend to keep my private life private and hate that this is all out in the open for everyone to see, and comment on."

"For what it's worth, I think your housemates are concerned for you and genuinely care. I doubt any of them for one second believe you're involved with Jackson's death."

"Thanks. I hope so. Me and my big mouth are what got me in trouble this time. But that man made me so damn angry!"

Nina's eyes slid to one side, and I followed her look. Of course, my raised voice had other diners looking our way. I'd never learn. I put my head down and poked at the last few bites on my plate. "Sorry."

"Well, you know what they say about the likes of Sloane Jackson, don't you?"

"Good riddance?" I volunteered, not at all in the mood for guessing games.

"Time wounds all heels."

I smirked at that. "Good one. Thanks, Nina. So, tell me, you said you had a change of heart, creating characters or a story, based on our charming little family back at the lodge?"

"Easy enough to do. I only had a basic outline of the story. But I guess in future, if I want to base a story on fact, I'd better not become fond of the people involved."

Before I could comment the server appeared to enquire about dessert. Nina wasn't quite ready and ordered more wine.

"We're not in a rush, are we?" She asked as the server moved away. "I'm enjoying this evening."

"No hurry for me, but, um, I'd hate to see you get a DUI."

"Don't you worry about me, chickie. This round's for you. Haven't you noticed?"

I sat back. She was right. I was the one emptying the bottle! She'd only had one glass.

"You might want to take a couple of headache pills before bed, hon. You're on track for one boomer of a headache come morning."

When the server returned with more wine, I asked her to bring a dessert menu and coffee. I couldn't believe I'd kicked back so much wine without noticing. Wine hangovers are the worst. But I couldn't let the fine vintage go to waste, could I?

Nina's smile confirmed she was enjoying my discomfort. "You've been pretty tense since that guy of yours arrived in town, and now with his death. Bet you're not feeling so tense now, right?"

"Correct, but I had no intention of drinking so much. Shit and this wine isn't cheap."

"My treat. Forget about it."

"But..."

"Tell me about what happened with Minnie today and I'll call it even?"

Minnie? Crap, the wine had caught up with me and fog was invading my brain. I wasn't supposed to talk about Minnie, was I? Why were the yellow stripes on her shirt rolling?

I was trying to form a cohesive reply when I noticed Alysha standing at our table. Where did she come from? She looked upset.

"Nina. You need to come home. It's Hemingway."

CHAPTER TWENTY-ONE
Alysha

That's all I needed. A sixty-something woman in the bag. Oh, Dianne. How much did you drink?

Nina and I each took an arm and helped her to her feet. Flashbacks of helping fellow students at university came to mind. Especially after I spied two empty bottles of wine amidst several food plates. They must have eaten enough to feed a small village!

Nina threw bills on the table for the server and proceeded to frantically fish for her car keys. Nervous energy spilled from her in waves. "What's happened to Hemingway? He was fine when I left, sleeping on his blankie. Oh, where the hell are my keys!"

"Chill, Nina. You can leave your car here for now. I'll need your help with Dianne anyway, so ride with us. C'mon on, let's go. We need to walk this lady to the car. Drowning her sorrows, was she?"

"I think she needed to unwind." She gave her purse one last shake and then we focused on getting Dianne, who was semi-conscious and for all intents and purposes legless, into my car.

Nina settled in the back seat, gave a last longing look at her car, and immediately returned to her priority. "Who found him?"

What a loaded question. I didn't want to detail any of the Minnie situation with Nina, so kept the answer to a bare minimum.

"Believe it or not, it was Minnie. She heard him throwing up I guess and went into your room. She's been with him ever since. I think you should get him to a vet, he seemed quite listless when I saw him."

"Minnie! That old crone has no love for my poor wee doggie."

Nina was right. Minnie wouldn't have been caught dead with her dog. But I couldn't think of a way to explain the change. Think! "Main thing is, Nina, someone was there when needed."

"Yes, of course. But what on earth could have made him sick?"

"I have no idea. And speaking of sick, I hope Dianne doesn't hurl before we get her back home." She'd nodded off to sleep and I crossed my fingers she'd stay that way a few minutes longer.

"Do you have the name of a vet?"

"You could try the clinic we use for the alpacas. I can't remember the name but search vets in Grant's Crossing. With luck, you'll find one who'll come to the lodge."

While Nina busied herself on her phone, I concentrated on the rest of the drive, and we were soon parked in the driveway. Jan must have been watching for us and opened the front door. The car had barely stopped before Nina sprang out and raced up the steps. As she flew past Jan, she cried, "Where's my baby?"

I doubt she even heard Jan reply, "In your room, with Minnie."

Jan came down the steps, shaking her head. "Her *baby*. Goodness, what a fuss. Now then, what's wrong with Dianne?"

I thought Jan might either have a fit, or burst out laughing, as she took in the spectacle of Dianne, head lolled to one side, and snoring. "It would appear she's had a bit too much wine, Jan. Can you help me get her to her room?"

I shook Dianne's shoulder to wake her. One eye opened, and she muttered, "Huh?"

"Welcome back to the land of the living. Think you can make it to your room if Jan and I help you?"

She rubbed at her eyes, blinked, and then tried to move. Her arms reached out to us. Jan, usually unflappable, wasn't a happy camper. I tried to placate her. "Cheer up, Jan. You know she'll suffer for this tomorrow."

Jan muttered something along the lines of not knowing what the place was coming to. "Dalton would never have stood for this. A dog being sick everywhere, drunk residents – what else?"

"Speaking of what else. While it's just us, Jan. Were you able to contact a doctor about Minnie?"

We were struggling to balance Dianne between us, and I thought Jan was about to answer my question, when my love arrived on the scene. Questions were written all over his face, but this wasn't the time or place to go into details.

"Babe, it's been an evening. I'll have to explain it all later. Hemingway's sick. A vet should be here shortly, so can you wait here and show him to Nina's room? Jan and I will get Dianne settled."

"Would you rather I help with Dianne?"

Jan bristled and waved him away. "We can manage perfectly fine. You wait here for the vet, thank you."

She apologised for her reaction to Jeff. "I'm sorry Alysha. I hope you don't mind if I prefer to speak about Minnie to just you?"

"Good call. Let's settle Dianne and then you can tell me."

We bundled Dianne onto the elevator and soon had her tucked into bed. She was out for the count.

"Okay, Jan tell me. What about Minnie?"

Jan looked about ready to cave. "You have no idea the hoops I needed to go through trying to get some help for her. I started making calls, then the fracas with Hemingway erupted and it meant I had to focus on that situation. Up until you came home, I've been on the phone. One call led to another, and then another. By the time I finally was referred to someone who would help, they told me nothing was available until the morning! I have an appointment to take her to a specialist at nine tomorrow."

"Oh, poor you. And then I had to leave to find Nina and Dianne. I should have been here with you as well."

"If we ever figure our cloning, little one, put me first in line." We shared a chuckle and then made sure Dianne had water and headache pills beside her bed.

From her room, we went to Nina's, which was a hive of activity. The vet had arrived and was examining Hemingway. Minnie stood off to one side, constantly pushing up and down the sleeves of her sweater. I caught Nina's eye and she stopped hovering over the vet and her dog. I recognized a look of relief on the vet's face as she moved away from him.

Nina's mascara had bled into large dark rings, and she kept biting her lip. "I'm so worried, my poor baby."

Truth be told I was more concerned about Minnie, but Nina needed to chill. Jan remained standing in the doorway, as if reluctant to be involved. Or she was intentionally leaving me in charge?

I'd figure it out later. Nina needed to compose herself. "Take a breath. How is he doing?"

"I don't know. I don't *know*. When I raced up here, I found Minnie cradling him in her arms. She was singing to him!" If Nina's voice rose any higher the ceiling would have to be raised.

Minnie started at the mention of her name but didn't move from her spot. She tore her eyes from the dog and spoke with genuine distress. "He was so sick. Poor thing, what a mess. I tried to calm him down."

What a day for Minnie. Without knowing what happened earlier, I'd bet Nina was baffled by this change in her behaviour. Minnie had only been nasty to Hemingway since day one. Nina approached Minnie and I was on full alert wondering what she'd say to her. What a turnaround for everyone.

As if not a bad word had ever been said between them Nina spoke to Minnie, "I want to thank you for comforting my precious until I got here. I think you've made a big difference in how he's feeling."

The vet had begun packing up his equipment and turned to face Nina. "I'd say Ms. Parker's quick thinking made a positive difference and averted a tragedy."

The scene felt surreal, and I asked, "Will he be okay?" I wasn't overly fond of the dog but didn't want to see him ill, or worse.

"I've taken samples to run tests and given him something to relax him. I'd say his system purged itself of disagreeable contents, and he should be fine. He needs to rest. Don't hesitate to call me if you need to. Otherwise, I'll call you tomorrow to follow up."

Nina returned to converse with the vet. I took Minnie aside. She was agitated and I feared a repeat of her earlier behaviour. I tried to be calm and spoke in a soft tone. "Are you okay? You did a good thing here tonight."

Her lip trembled. "I heard him, being sick, you know. Whimpering and crying - he was all alone. So, I went in to see. I called for Jan, and she came, too."

I already knew how Minnie had found the dog, but I let her repeat the story. It seemed important for her to tell it.

Nina bounced back and forth between the vet and us. She came back with yet another unsolicited accolade for Minnie. I thought she was going to hug her dog's rescuer, but she backed off at the last second. "Minnie took great care of him. I had a hard time prying him from your arms, didn't I?"

Minnie blinked, "Babies need comforting when they're sick. They need their mothers."

Before Nina could ask, I reached for one of Minnie's hands. "How about I take you to your room. I can get you a cup of tea if you like?"

"Okay." She offered no resistance.

We turned to leave the room, but not before I heard Nina say to Hemingway, "Mummy's here now, precious. We'll have to find out why Minnie thought you were a baby, won't we?"

I closed the door behind us. Nina's curiosity had surfaced. I'd worry about it later.

By the time I settled Minnie with a cup of tea, it was well after eight o'clock and dusk had fallen. I joined Jeff and Jan, who waited for me in the front room. Thankfully Jan had managed to head off any questions from the other residents about the commotion around Hemingway. We'd already had to pacify concerns around Minnie's well being. The day better not have any more surprises.

Jan had set out a tray with coffee and pastries. I was happy with the coffee but bet Jeff would have preferred a beer. At least we had a few chilling in our space upstairs; he'd survive.

And she had an opinion on what had made the dog ill. "Before she and Dianne went out, she let him wander around near the flower beds. That woman must think the rules apply to everyone but her! She'd let him dig around in the gardens and it looked like he'd been chewing on different plants. And when she saw me, she pulled him away, looking as if she had no idea he'd been where he wasn't allowed."

Jeff nodded. "Maybe she's convinced now that he should only be in the run Frank and I built."

"Let's hope so, babe. And I'm making it a rule in future – no pets!"

Jan smiled. "I'm relieved to hear that. Thank you, little one." She finished her coffee and looked at me. "Tonight was another interruption for you, wasn't it?"

I sighed. "Don't I know it. I'd just laid out paperwork on all things real estate to prepare for a meeting with a broker. And then the chaos broke out! I'm starting to wonder if my idea of getting into real estate is a fruitless venture."

"Your meeting is tomorrow? Is Dax going with you to handle the introductions?" asked Jan. Beside me, Jeff ever so slightly tensed up. Dax had become something of a sore point between us.

"My appointment is for one o'clock. Things better have settled down by then because there's no way I want to postpone this meeting."

Jeff murmured. "If it's meant to be, everything will work out."

I leaned into him and was about to speak when Nina peeked into the room. "Alysha. Sorry, I don't mean to intrude, but wondering if I could get a ride back into town to get my car? I don't like leaving it overnight."

Jeff stood. "I can take you. Alysha's had a pretty full day."

"No, Jeff, but thanks. I was the one who suggested she leave her car, so I'll take her." I smiled at him. "I think there's a cold brew waiting for you upstairs?"

Jan began gathering the cups and tidying up. "Is the dog okay to leave, Nina?"

"He's sleeping in his bed. The vet said he'd likely not stir for hours, so that's why I thought it might be a good time to go now. Or I can get a cab."

Her usual bravado was absent, and she looked spent. While it would have been a good opportunity to remind her that the gardens were a dog-free area, I didn't have the heart and instead confirmed I'd drive her into town. "I'll be with you in ten minutes, okay?"

"Thank you. I'll go grab my purse."

She left and our threesome broke up.

***

It was nearly nine-thirty before we left, and the restaurant would have been closed for a while. Nina was quiet on the ride, and I let her be. We pulled into the near-empty parking lot, and I drew alongside her pride and joy.

Nina had her hand on the door when a flash of movement caught my eye. "Hey! Someone's trying to get into your car!"

Nina flew out the door before I could tell her to wait, and she bounded to the driver's side of her car. I was fast on her heels. She whipped her purse at the hooded head of a person crouched near the door lock. My brain, trying to catch up, wondering why he hadn't heard us drive in.

Nina screeched, "Get away from my car!" Then bashed at him again. He stumbled sideways, and kicked at her, connecting with her shin, judging by the yelp she produced.

In the struggle, his hood fell back. He was only a kid. I yelled at him to stop hitting her.

"Tell *her*, man! She's hurting me. Stop!"

I reached for Nina's arm before she landed another hit. "Nina, stop!"

She backed up and caught her breath. Which was enough time for the culprit to scramble to his feet and take off running. He ducked into nearby shrubbery and disappeared.

I kept hold of her arm. She was trembling and wild-eyed. I was shaking, too, but needed her to calm down. "He's gone, Nina. Breathe. I'm going to call the cops."

She slumped against her car and let her purse drop to the ground. "Little pissant. I got a good look at him." Then she turned to peer at her car's door. "If he's scratched this..."

"Don't touch anything until the cops get here. There might be prints."

"Good point. Guess I won't make a crime writer after all."

"Didn't you say you need to write what you know? Well, you're going to have first-hand experience with a crime scene, because here comes the police."

***

Another late night. Nearly midnight before Nina and I arrived home. Still without her car. The officer wasn't going to impound it, but they wanted to wait till daylight to search the area. She'd likely have the car back mid-morning. And the police seemed impressed with the description we were able to provide of the would-be thief.

Have I mentioned there's never a dull moment around here? Today had been one for the books. A real hat trick. First Minnie's breakdown, then Hemingway, and now this.

Jeff had promised to wait up for me. I entered our apartment to see him finishing up an episode of his favourite program – *The Walking Dead*. Kind of appropriate because I was starting to feel like a zombie myself, although I had no desire to watch it.

I leaned over the couch and kissed the top of his head. "Is it too late to have a beer?"

He turned off the TV. "Let's sit on the balcony and I'll bring us a couple."

Good idea. I passed the table where all my untouched real estate paperwork lay. Was I never going to see this career get off the ground?

After I gave him the details about Nina and her car, I felt I could finally relax. We sat in silence for a while, watching the stars. A beautiful summer evening. Deceptively quiet after the day's events.

But I needed to get a few things off my chest. "Babe, I need to talk to you. I know how important the alpacas are to you, and our future. But if I ever get my real estate business up and running, I need to know I can depend on you to be in charge in my absence. Today was a perfect example."

The moonlight softened his face. "Aly, I do care for the alpacas, but you are my only love and my priority. I know I need kicking sometimes to get back on track, but whatever you need, I'm here."

My heart melted, and I was reassured I could face anything as long as Jeff was on board. "You're the best."

"Of course, because it's only the best for my girl. Now I think it's time to call it a night. You have that meeting tomorrow."

"Right. I may not be here when the vet calls. Who knows what that little devil ate in the garden."

"Babe. Turn it off. We'll let tomorrow take care of itself. You need to sleep."

He was right. The day was done and dusted, as my grandmother would say. I hoped the worst thing we'd deal with the next day would be Dianne's hangover.

CHAPTER TWENTY-TWO
Dianne

Who was pounding on the walls at sun-up? I forced one eye open, the other still held in place with my pillow, and saw rays of sunlight darting across my ceiling. The pounding was in my head, and I groaned. I shut my eyes again and took inventory. Head booming, tongue replaced with a dry sponge, and stomach rolling. Damn. Hangover.

Memories of the night before took shape and I forced myself to focus on them until they ended with me looking at Alysha standing over our table. Not for anything could I remember much after that. Vague awareness of being helped out of Alysha's car with Jan, maybe? Then lights out.

I hated hangovers. I couldn't remember the last one I'd had. Certainly not since I'd lived here. I forced myself to move and hung my legs over the bed. My stomach would dictate how fast I'd be moving and in which direction. Then apprehension raised its ugly head. What had I told Nina last night? She'd asked about Minnie, I think. I remember we talked about Sloane.

I took a deep breath and made my feet connect with the floor. Steady on, and I felt my stomach would hold. It was my head that made me want to curl up in a ball.

I heard a timid knock at my door. "Dianne? Are you awake? It's Nina. I have coffee."

Magic words. I shuffled to the door and opened it a crack. A sympathetic face greeted me as did the aroma of a fresh cup of java. "Can I come in?"

I was grateful she spoke just above a whisper, and I cautiously nodded.

"You poor thing. I should take some of the blame. I bring a peace offering." She held the coffee up, and I took it.

I had to take a sip of liquid before my mouth would function. "Thanks. What time is it?"

"Almost ten. You've missed breakfast, so I thought I'd come to check on you and give you the latest news."

"Have a seat, but no lights. Please."

She chuckled and sat. I returned to the edge of my bed and managed a few more welcome sips of brew before I ventured to speak again.

My eyes finally seemed to be working as they should, and the pounding had lessened. "What's the latest news? I barely remember getting home last night? In Alysha's car?"

"Oh, I've got news for you alright. Yes, Alysha brought us home. Jan helped her get you to bed. Do you remember anything about Hemingway?"

"Is that why Alysha was at the restaurant? Why didn't she call us - we had our phones?"

"We'd put them on silent, remember?" She proceeded to tell me what had happened to her *baby*. I had a feeling there was a little embellishment on her rendition, but I wasn't in the mood to quibble. I was surprised to learn of Minnie's role in saving the dog. "And Hemingway's okay now?"

"He seems to be fine this morning." She turned to study some prints on my wall. "Um, it appears he ate something disagreeable in one of the gardens. According to the vet, he nearly died. And it was my fault. Jan did tell me to keep him away from the flowers. But how was I to know some of them were poisonous to a dog?"

Nina couldn't stay contrite for long. And I didn't have the energy to take her to task. "Could have been worse, then? I'm glad he's okay."

"Thanks, chickie. But there's more." Her voice had risen, and I raised a hand so she'd back off a bit.

"Sorry. The evening didn't end there. After my snookums settled, Alysha drove me back to get my car. And guess what? Someone was trying to steal it and we stopped him!"

When she mentioned her car, visions of eye-piercing yellow stabbed at my brain, and I flinched. She misunderstood.

"Oh, we didn't get hurt. I managed a couple of good clips to his head, and he took off."

"Wow," was about all I could manage. "Did the police come?"

"Yes, and we were able to give them a good description of the kid." She sat back with a satisfied look on her face. Civic duty to the max.

I finished the rest of my coffee, and while I was grateful she'd brought it to me, I needed to sort myself out. "Thanks again for the coffee. Headache's a bit better, but I need to take a shower."

"Oh, of course." She stood to leave and reached for the empty mug. "One more thing. That nice constable, Detective Young, called and said he'd be coming by later to talk with you."

I clapped my hand to my mouth and ran for the bathroom.

***

I finally made my way back to reality just after noon. Sunglasses were perfect to hide my eyes' evidence of how I felt, and I longed to find a quiet spot on the veranda and soak up the warmth of the sun. The thought of any food brought on nausea. I was content to sip on a ginger-ale until my stomach settled.

I was relieved to see I had the veranda to myself. The air was warm, and I closed my eyes. I kept them closed when I heard the door open a couple of times. If I feigned sleep, I hoped no one would bother me. But I couldn't ignore the gentle pressure on my arm and a voice that whispered, "Dianne?"

Alysha once again stood over me. Deja vu from the previous evening, and for one brief moment I thought I was back in the restaurant. She didn't look unsympathetic, but I was embarrassed at my behaviour.

"Hi." I sat up straighter. "Listen, I have to apologize for my condition last night. I don't remember a lot about getting home, but I understand you helped put me to bed. Thanks."

She sat down next to me. "I imagine how you're feeling this morning is punishment enough. I won't add to it."

"Thanks, I think."

"At least you kept your hair on."

I laughed when I recalled the last drunk she'd helped to bed had been Ty. His hairpiece had nearly slipped off his head, and her comment encouraged me to think she was in a forgiving mood.

"I guess you heard someone from the police department is coming here in a bit. More questions I'm afraid, or maybe it's good news on your car."

"Yes, Nina told me earlier. I think I should call the lawyer she recommended, just in case."

Worry lines creased Alysha's forehead. "Whatever happened to innocent until proven guilty? I know it's upsetting, Dianne, but I have faith the truth will come to light. Unfortunately, I won't be here when the police arrive to offer moral support."

That's when I noticed she was dressed for business and had a portfolio by her feet. I reassured her I'd be fine. "Long as Jan is around to stand guard." The attempted joke was as flat as my ginger-ale, and I couldn't pretend I wasn't apprehensive. "So, looks like you're off to a meeting?"

Her smile lit up her face, and her curls bounced to match her enthusiasm.

"Yes! I'm finally meeting Bennett Howes. He's the biggest realtor in the area and he's agreed to talk about mentoring me with my real estate career. I'm nervous and excited, all at the same time!"

"Good for you, kiddo. You'll be fine. Grant's Crossing could use some new blood in the real estate business, too. I'll be here when you get back and want to know all about it. Promise."

"You better be. Oh, and one more thing. You were still sleeping this morning, but Jan managed to have a doctor see Minnie. She's going to be hospitalized for a while and get the help she needs. She was a godsend though last night with Hemingway. Who'd have believed it. I'll tell you more later, but I really have to run!"

She thanked me again and ran down the steps to her car. As I watched her drive away, I could only hope I'd be able to keep my promise to be here when she returned.

CHAPTER TWENTY-THREE
Alysha

I've often been nervous in unfamiliar situations, but since taking on Leven Lodge and all its variables, I've toughened up a bit. I think.

But right now, trying to settle on one train of thought was next to impossible. I fought not to feel resentment where Minnie was concerned. I'd only wanted to focus on my meeting with Bennett Howes.

While I finished preparing for the meeting, I played back my talk with Jan earlier. I'd been strung out and gone to the kitchen for a coffee. Dianne was still sleeping, and Jeff was busy. I had no one to talk with, so I wandered into the kitchen.

I had poured my coffee and wondered how Jan was doing. She'd left earlier, taking Minnie to see a specialist. Would there be good news for our eccentric resident?

I'd only taken one sip, when I heard Jan's voice. Thank goodness they were back. "In here," I called.

When Jan entered the kitchen, she was alone.

"Where's Minnie?"

My friend looked drained, and I made her sit. I pushed a cup of coffee in front of her and sat down with her.

"What happened? Will she be alright?"

Jan held the mug and didn't speak for a few moments. I didn't like the dark circles under her eyes. My selfish side feared Jan would not be able to cope with much more. How would I manage if she decided to quit? I mentally scolded myself.

"Jan? Talk to me."

"If I thought advocating for the McTaggarts had been rough, this was - pardon my language - hell."

Strong stuff coming from Jan, and I didn't interrupt.

She sighed and sipped at her coffee. "They feel she has had a long overdue psychotic break - at least from their initial assessment. Years of unresolved emotions never properly dealt with. And that's just scratching the surface."

"I have a feeling this is on a bigger scale than Philips's breakdown?"

She managed a small laugh. "Maybe there's something in the water around here?"

I hated feeling useless. Jan bore the brunt of everything unpleasant. "Oh, Jan. I am sorry you had to deal with this by yourself. I take it she's been admitted for care?"

She only nodded, and a tear ran down her cheek. "Poor Minnie. I should have been more aware. Not like there weren't signs over the years."

"Stop, Jan. You're not a doctor. I believe Minnie had the best possible home here with you and my grandmother. Don't ever forget that. And we'll be here for her when she's better. Won't we?"

Jan patted my hand. "I promise if you do as well. Of course, at this point there's no way to tell how long she'll be away. The doctor was encouraged, though, by Minnie's acceptance that she needed help. And she even said she'd do whatever the doctor said to get well."

What a relief! Not that Minnie wasn't coming home, but that she was willing to get the help she needed.

I had been so torn listening to her and hoped she would understand. "I hate to be a kill-joy, Jan, but I need to get ready for my meeting with Bennett Howes."

"Off you go. I think I'll take a short walk outside and then see about dinner plans. On the bright side, this will be a great opportunity to give her room a thorough cleaning and maybe some fresh paint."

"We are holding it for her?"

"Absolutely. Minnie belongs here as much as anyone."

***

I'd agreed to meet Dax in the coffee shop near Bennett Howes' office, and I arrived early to grab a table. I hadn't seen Dax since Dianne's car towing incident. He'd been all business that day, the polar opposite to his behaviour at the barbecue. I didn't care for the uncomfortable vibes he gave off that evening. Seemed I couldn't get a handle on him, which made me speculate on the mood he'd been in today.

I conceded to myself that a little flirting might be good for the ego, but I didn't want him coming on to me. Or have expectations because he was connecting me with Bennet Howes.

"Alysha, hi." My musings were cut short as Dax settled into the seat opposite, coffee and muffin in hand. I refrained from commenting on the cop stereotype. "Need a refill?"

"No, thanks. I'll wait till after the meeting, don't think I'd do it justice right now."

"Case of nerves?" He smiled and those eyes made my heart falter for a brief second.

"A little, maybe. I am anxious to know if I have any kind of future in real estate. And I do appreciate your referral, thanks again."

He reached a hand to touch mine. "That's what friends are for."

I pulled mine away, but my skin tingled where he'd touched it. "Speaking of friends, how come I'm Alysha today and not Ms. Grant?"

He wiped muffin crumbs from his mouth and swallowed more coffee. "You know when I'm on duty it's cop first. Being social comes second."

Of course, he was right. I must have sounded petty and needed to play it cool. "Makes sense. Say, we have a few minutes before the meeting. Any news on Sloane Jackson's murder, or Dianne?"

He raised an eyebrow. "Listen, I know she's your friend. This is a serious crime and I wonder just how well you know her. Only for about a year, right?"

"What's that supposed to mean?"

"I think the question is obvious, isn't it?"

What was with this guy? A straight answer would have been nice. "I only asked because I believe someone from your department is coming to see her. Right about now, I think. I'd say I know her a lot better than I know you. No way she had anything to do with his death!"

He held up a hand. "Point taken. I apologize. Chalk it up to the difference in our points of view."

Why was it so easy for him to get under my skin? "So, do you have news or not?"

He didn't seem rattled by the demanding tone of my voice, which only served to irritate me further! He smiled and sipped at his coffee.

"Dax! Stop prolonging the agony. Tell me."

He pushed his empty cup aside. Teasing from Jeff is one thing, but this was fast becoming annoying. "I do have some news. However, most of it I'm unable to share with you, understood?"

I nodded, "And?"

"Dubois should be there now with good news for Dianne. Some points to clarify and I'm optimistic she'll be cleared of any wrongdoing."

Relief washed over me. "Thank God. What other points, though?"

"Alysha."

"Right, sorry. And she'll get her car back. Wait! Does this mean you have a suspect in custody?"

"You're like a dog with a bone. Yes, to the car, and no comment to the rest." He glanced at his watch. "We should get a move on. Once I introduce you, I'll be on my way."

Smooth way to change the subject. I played nice as we left the coffee shop on our way to Howes' office. "What can you tell me about him?"

"Bennett? The unofficial king of real estate in Grant's Crossing. Been here since before I was born. Good reputation, no complaints that I'm aware of. Gets involved with town activities to promote Grant's Crossing, and himself. Knows his stuff. Trust me, if I didn't think he was above-board, I wouldn't have referred you." He paused and his next comment was more to himself than me. "Kind of a man's man."

Ugh. That didn't impress me at all. I let it slide because we'd arrived at our destination.

"But I'll let you make up your mind. And for what it's worth, Ms. Grant, you'll be a success at whatever you put your imagination too. I hope Jeff realizes how lucky he is."

Thankfully, there was no time for my response; Dax held open the door for me and we entered Bennett Howes' kingdom.

One wall displayed a multitude of current real estate listings. In front sat a receptionist, busy with a teetering stack of files. Somewhere a phone was ringing. The atmosphere blared success and activity.

I'd seen the likeness of Bennett Howes from lawn signs around town but was unprepared for him in the flesh.

About sixty, tall and paunchy. His florid face said high blood pressure or too many drinks, The comb-over was an out-of-place touch. Well-dressed, he oozed confidence. An overly large gold ring pressed into my palm as we shook hands.

"Ms. Grant. Pleased to finally meet you. Thank you, Dakotah, for arranging this."

"My pleasure." And with that, Dax, and his mixed messages, left.

"Let's go to my office." He pointed to an open door, and I moved ahead of him into a room that screamed testosterone overload. A large, antique, oak desk dominated the room and seemed out of context with the sleek computer equipment on a matching credenza.

And here I was again, in the offices of a male anachronism, who showed no hesitation in giving me the once-over. I gritted my teeth. And remembered I'd once thought similarly about my lawyer, Bryce Lockhart. We were very good friends, now. I'd have to give old Bennett a chance.

I sat across from the desk, and he lowered his large frame into a well-worn leather chair, where he folded his age-spotted hands over his belly.

"Thank you for seeing me today. I'll try not to take up your time. Looks like you're pretty busy. Business must be good?"

"It's very good, young lady. And I'm delighted to have this meeting. Both Dakotah and Janelle speak highly of you. It's a wonder we haven't bumped into each other before now."

"And I have to say your reputation precedes you."

He bellowed with laughter and leaned forward. I squirmed under his scrutiny, and the lingering scent of cigar, but wouldn't give him the satisfaction of showing how much it bothered me.

"Ms. Grant – Alysha – I like your style. Straight forward, no-nonsense. We'll leave details of my reputation for when we know each other a little better, shall we? And please call me Bennett."

Boy, I was glad the door to his office stood open.

"So, down to business." He pulled a file toward him and tapped it. "I've reviewed your resume. More than adequate for this neck of the woods." He leaned back. "A resume is on paper. I want to know about *you*. How you handle Leven Lodge and its occupants. Not what you anticipated back in your University of Guelph days, I'd say."

"It's been an adjustment, but I am enjoying my new responsibilities. My partner, Jeff, is a tremendous help. And Jan is the one who ensures everything runs smoothly." I hoped he wouldn't ask about Ty Rogers or the recent death of Sloane Jackson. I kept talking to avoid any interruption. "It keeps me busy, but I love challenges. Which is why I'm here."

"Of course. I see you have your real estate license, but no experience to date. I can imagine Leven Lodge keeps you hopping. Will you have the time needed to devote to real estate? Clients can be demanding, calling at all hours for example. Are you prepared for that?"

"I guarantee you, Bennett, Jeff is fully on board with my plans and knows he'll have to cover for me whenever it's needed."

"I can be an exacting teacher as well."

I hoped there was no hidden agenda behind that statement. But forewarned is forearmed, or something like that.

"Eventually I'll bring another staffer on board at the lodge to also assist in the day-to-day chores as needed."

Bennett nodded and seemed satisfied with my plan. "All very commendable, Alysha. Tell me, what do you envision for the real estate business, specifically here in Grant's Crossing, over the next ten years or so?"

Excellent question and one I had given thought to. But I didn't want to appear anxious, or a know-it-all.

"You know I lived here as a child, but of course children don't notice much beyond their world. However, when I returned last year, I became aware of the wonderful architecture of so many homes. I'm gratified to know that the town works hard to preserve the history and heritage of these homes."

"Our Heritage Society is very proud of the work they do. I sit on their board and will pass on your comments."

My confidence strengthened with his remarks, and I forged ahead. "That being said, Grant's Crossing is primed for housing growth. It's inevitable as people move away from larger urban centres to a quieter lifestyle. A case in point is the new Rivermill Resort. Other businesses will open to support the growth as well. Tourism will grow and some will decide to become permanent residents. I see only good things happening here and I want to be part of it. Grant's Crossing is a wonderful place to call home."

I sat back, wondering if I'd said too much because he was silent. Then he stood and walked over the large window. An awkward silence threatened to dampen my enthusiasm. Had I said something wrong? I waited.

"Alysha. I'm impressed with your ability to understand growth is essential for Grant's Crossing to thrive. I see we're on the same page and I would be pleased and honoured to be your mentor in this business. What I don't know about real estate in Grant's Crossing could be put on the back of a postage stamp!"

"Are you sure? This is wonderful. Thank you! When can we start?"

"Slow down a bit. How about next Monday? By then I'll clear some office space for you."

He beamed at me, and I ran the risk of blubbering my gratitude. There wasn't much more to be said and I didn't want to say thank you ten more times. What I did want was to rush home and share the news with Jeff. So, I stood and with tremendous effort, kept my voice calm. "I'll see you next Monday. Thank you so much." Okay, one more slipped out, I couldn't help it.

I left the office, trying not to skip, or click my pretend ruby heels together. Potential business names raced through my mind but halted when *Alysha Grant – Stand Fast Real Estate* came to the forefront. I'd just found the pot of gold for my rainbow.

CHAPTER TWENTY-FOUR
Dianne

By mid-afternoon, the hangover had subsided to a manageable level. Tentative hunger pangs were present, leading me to the kitchen in search of a light snack.

The kitchen was spotless. Jan was a fastidious housekeeper; no self-respecting speck of dirt would be found within range of her. I wasn't much of a Suzy homemaker, but I respected her efforts and did my best to clean up after myself.

I put together a small snack and decided to take a walk out back near the barn. I hadn't been out there for a while and the alpacas could make me smile.

Jeff and Philip were deep in conversation, and I let them be. The sun felt good, and I made short work of the crackers and cheese I'd brought along. I leaned over the paddock fence and spied the herd relaxing under the shade of several trees. Two of the group were pregnant and due soon. But for the life of me, I couldn't tell which ones they were. According to Jeff, because alpacas are prey animals, nature designed them to hide any weaknesses. And a big belly would be a definite sign of weakness to a predator. I guess nature knows what it's doing.

A slight breeze had risen, and for the first time in the last week, I felt at peace and content.

"Dianne!"

The bubble burst. Jan's voice had an urgency to it that meant only one thing. Reality had returned to confront me. "Here you are. You need to come back to the house. The police are here."

Contentment fled with anxiety's advance. Jan's face reflected the worry I felt. We walked back toward the house. "Are they inside, or should I just go around to the front?"

"Inside. It's only Dubois this time, but I'll stay with you."

DC Steven Dubois waited for us in the front room. I searched his face for hints behind this visit. Briefly, I thought I knew how a person on trial must feel waiting on a jury's verdict. Bile rose in my throat, and I willed my stomach to settle.

"Can I get anyone a coffee? Glass of water?" Jan's offer met with head shakes.

"I won't be taking much of your time, ladies." And finally, the slightest smile appeared on his face. He held out his hand to me. "Your keys, Ms. Mitchell. You can pick up your car anytime."

I accepted them with gratitude. "That's a relief. Do you have any more news for me?"

"Not a lot I'm able to share with you, but I can tell you this. We have sent all of Mr. Jackson's financial information - business and personal - to a forensics accountant. Let's just say it became obvious to us there are glaring inconsistencies with what we saw that deserve a detailed look. It points in your favour. However, you are still required to stay in town, got it?"

"You give me back my car and tell me to stay put?" I put on a mock pout and hoped the levity would not be a mark against me. "Not fair, Detective."

He laughed. "Not fair, but necessary."

"Anything else you can tell us?" Jan's voice held the optimistic note I needed to hear.

"I have a question for Ms. Mitchell."

"Of course, whatever I can do to help." Was the tide turning for me on this?

He flipped pages in his notebook. "The day you say Mr. Jackson approached you in the Crossings Tavern, was he alone?"

"As I recall he came in with two other men. But I only glanced at them because my attention was focused on Sloane."

"Can you describe them?"

Here we go again. Do people never listen to what you've just said! "I'm sorry, no. Other than to say I think they were younger than Sloane, dressed in business casual. Why?"

Typical police routine – he ignored my question. "And you were with Mrs. Edwards at the time - do you think she could provide any description?" He didn't wait for an answer but requested Jan find Rose and bring her to us.

Jan left and we waited in silence. My back was up a bit at Dubois' demanding tone. Assuming Rose would be on hand, assuming she knows anything. I gritted my teeth so I wouldn't voice my thoughts and undo the ground I'd gained.

Rose soon appeared – a fresh coat of red lipstick and all. That colour! Really, Rose - *really*?

She threw on the charm. "Detective. How nice to see you again."

"You as well, Mrs. Edwards. I just need you to answer a question or two if you don't mind. It's about the day in the tavern when Mr. Jackson accosted Ms. Mitchell. There were two other men with him that day. Can you describe them?"

Rose looked at me for a second, then geared up with her answer. "To be honest, Detective, my back was to them, and if I'm being truthful – which I always am, of course – I wasn't even aware of them until your mention of them just now. I had the impression Mr. Jackson was there by himself."

Dubois scribbled in his notebook. "I see. Okay, thank you. If either of you finds you suddenly remember anything about these other two men, please let us know. Understood?"

Trust me, if I somehow recalled seeing one of them had a hangnail, I'd be letting the police know. Anything to get the focus away from me.

He put his pen and notebook away. "I think that's all for now, ladies. Thank you for your help and we'll be in touch if we need anything further."

He left. I couldn't be sure if I was off the hook or waiting to be reeled in. Judging from my companion's faces, they felt the same way.

I shrugged and tried to make light of the situation. "All good things come to those who wait. Or something like that, right?"

Rose hugged me. "I'm sorry I couldn't have been more helpful."

"It's okay, Rose. I'm only grateful you were with me that day. But look!" I jiggled my car keys at her, and she smiled.

Jan began untying her apron. "I bet you'd like a ride into town to get your car?"

Her offer was better than sympathy, any day. "Let's roll, Ms. Young."

We left just as Alysha returned, one question on her mind. "Where's Jeff?" She was beaming and full of energy. It would seem her interview in town had gone well, and while I was curious, it was clear she wanted to see Jeff first.

"The barn, as usual, with Philip."

"I should have guessed. Oh, and thanks, Dianne."

"What for?"

"Keeping your promise that you'd be here when I got back!"

My eyes teared up and I could only nod. I'd do anything to keep Leven Lodge as my home.

CHAPTER TWENTY-FIVE
Alysha

I entered the barn with a spring in my step and yelled out to Jeff who was doing whatever he does with hay for his *babies*. Wearing earbuds, I assumed he was listening to his usual headbanging music and hadn't heard me enter the barn. I waved frantically until he finally noticed me and took the buds out. He stopped what he was doing.

"Well, don't you look like the cat that got the cream."

"Jeff, I did it! I aced the interview with Bennett. He's agreed to mentor me in setting up as a broker. Starting Monday! I will have my own office and, oh I'm so excited. I'm on my way. *Alysha Grant – Stand Fast Real Estate* How does that sound?"

He came over and put his arms around me. A good place to be. "Congratulations, babe, you deserve this chance. I'll help out whenever I can get away from looking after the alpacas. And I have news for *you*."

Jeff plonked himself down on a big bale of hay, took my hand, and pulled me down beside him. I deflated. I was so excited to discuss my news, and as had happened far too often, he stole my thunder. I knew it wasn't intentional, but it was a bad habit he had. And to say *whenever he could get away from the alpacas* minimized my sense of worth!

Annoyance crept into my voice, and I couldn't help a sigh of exasperation. "What's your news, then? Can it be as important as what I've just told you?" My throat tightened as I fought back tears. "You have a way of discounting my accomplishments as if they're insignificant compared to yours, and it hurts."

The smile left his face. "Aly, I'm sorry you feel that way." He kissed me. "Of course, your news is wonderful, but I thought you would like to know that Junebug is in labour! I've sent for Rick, but he says not to worry, she'll do it all by herself."

Okay, that was worthy news. Now I was the one who felt churlish. "Oh, that is exciting news. We both have terrific reasons to be excited, but labour trumps real estate. At least for today." I hated bad feelings between us. Relationships require compromise - not always easy, and we still had lots to learn. "We can talk real estate later. Right now, I'm here to help you. What about Mags? Isn't this too early for them to be giving birth?"

I'd struck the right note. Boyish enthusiasm lit up his face. "C'mon, let's head to the meadow and see how she's doing. Mags is out there as well and when we see her, I'll try to answer your questions. I may be a novice with alpacas giving birth, but right after you left this morning, I noticed she showed signs of an early delivery."

I'd never seen a cria being born so this was a thrilling day. In fact, other than chickens hatching, I'd never seen any animal give birth. We walked quietly and kept our distance from the mum-to-be. We watched as she lay down briefly and then got up and walked for a bit.

I whispered, "She looks restless, or like she can't get comfortable."

He nodded and pointed at the others. They didn't seem interested at all - more absorbed in chewing their hay over by the shelter. Jeff was restless, too, and looked as if he was about to explode with excitement.

I started when a hand tapped my shoulder. Rick had arrived and spoke in low tones. "I'll examine her and see how she's progressing. Try to stay still so she's not startled. Like you, this is her first time, too." The smile he gave Jeff eased any anxiety I'd been feeling. Rick knew the ropes and we'd follow his lead. Even if it was only to observe.

I watched as he slowly moved over to Junebug, who again decided to lay down. He spoke softly to her all the while. Over his shoulder, he told us she looked to be in control and events were progressing as expected.

Rick moved his hands over Junebug's belly and walked around her. Mum was having none of it. She twitched and shook him off as if to say *Get lost, I can do this myself.* She lumbered to her feet again and walked away from him. Then laid back down again. This dance went on for some time.

Finally, Rick gave a thumbs up. "You can come closer, the show's about to start."

We crept in for a better view. Junebug seemed past the point of caring she was on display. As we drew closer, I could hear a humming sound. Rick must have noticed the puzzled look on my face. "The louder the hum from her, the closer the delivery. Won't be long now."

We backed up a bit as Junebug once more struggled to her feet.

"She may give birth standing," said Jeff. His voice held a note of awe I'd never heard before.

I was vaguely aware Frank and Philip had joined us. Philip, thankfully, had no words of wisdom to share, but no doubt he'd have comments later. I think we were all mesmerized by what was unfolding before us.

I'd never had maternal yearnings for a baby of my own, but seeing this miracle...

We didn't have to wait much longer. Rick and Jeff stood near in case their help was needed.

Jeff took his eyes away for a few seconds as the other alpacas sauntered over. "Oh look, here come the nosy ones but not Mags. I guess she doesn't want to see what's ahead for her!"

Our original alpacas, Larry, Moe, and Curly, came closer as if to offer support along with us. I couldn't help smiling as I watched their curious faces sniff the emerging baby. Spindly legs were all I saw at first, and sometimes my view was blocked.

Rick's excited but controlled voice alerted us. "And here she - or he - is. Your first cria Jeff, and what a perfect beauty."

The newborn tried to raise its wobbly head. Then it struggled to its feet and flopped back down. Junebug got down to the business of being a mother. I looked at my male companions, and to a one, all sported face splitting grins. No surprise and I'm sure I did as well.

Rick's voice of experience broke through the moment. "Let's back off and let mum bond with her. We'll check the cria out after mum has had some time with her new baby."

It was unfamiliar territory for me, and I was concerned for their well-being. "Should we move her to a pen? Away from the others?"

"Maybe, if any of them interfere. We can move them inside later if need be and after she's rested."

Jeff could not stop grinning. "This has been quite a day." He slapped Rick on the shoulder. "Thanks for your help and advice. And to my beautiful girl, Alysha. Did you know she'll soon be the real estate guru of Grant's Crossing?"

Jeff proceeded to fill the others in on my pending career in real estate. To me, it felt like he was offering crumbs after the banquet. What was wrong with me?

We broke up after all the congratulations were exhausted. Frank and Phillip lingered to watch over our newest arrival. Rick headed for his truck and shouted over his shoulder. "Congrats farmer Iverson. Now you know what to expect so I'd keep an eye on Mags as I don't think she'll be too long in giving your cria a brother or sister... Or are they cousins?"

We chuckled at his comment and made our way back to the house to tell the others the news. I needed to talk to Dianne and find out how Nina's *baby* was feeling today.

Wow - the day had flown by and now it was after four o'clock. Dinner time was fast approaching and with all that had happened today, I wondered if Jan knew who to expect for mealtime. I thought I'd better let her know Philip, who was first on cria watch with Mags, would probably be absent. Dinner would not be enough enticement to pull him away.

When Jeff and I breezed into the kitchen, she was there. Dinner preparations were well underway. She stopped peeling potatoes and looked at us with an eager face.

I let Jeff tell the story as he was so pleased you'd think he'd given birth himself. After the excitement died down about our cria and the soon-to-be arrival of another I gave her my news.

Jan beamed. "This is wonderful, Alysha. You do the Grant's proud, and I know your Uncle Dalton would be pleased as punch. And how was Bennett? He can be so full of himself but nothing you can't handle."

"I know what you mean. By the way, he sent you his regards. I don't know him well enough yet to provide an opinion but I'm grateful for the opportunity to learn from him."

"Hmm, sent his *regards, did* he!" She lowered her voice and beckoned me closer as if to share a long-held secret. Her smile had me believe she meant to tease, at least a little. "He was sweet on me back in the day, but I wasn't interested."

And that was all she revealed before her voice returned to normal. "I don't doubt you will learn from him, though. He's a successful realtor and knows his business."

I smiled at the woman of whom I've become very fond. Another tale of romance? I loved to tease her as well. "Right, Jan. Is this a dark side we don't know about? I want to hear more, but it will have to keep until later."

She smiled back at me. "Dark side? As if!"

"Well, it's a good thing you're in the middle of meal preparation, and I have things to do, or I'd be pumping for information!" I was about to leave when I remembered to ask, "Any update on Hemingway? I guess I should find Nina and see how they both are. I'm no fan of her dog, but I don't like to see animals in distress either.

"You'll be relieved to know he was tearing about in his run after lunch and seems to have perked up. Nina was looking for you, too. I believe she's heard from the vet and may have test results."

"Okay, I'll find her. But first I must see Dianne. I ran past her when I got home, and she knows I have news."

Jan nodded. "Good. I won't say anything, but she has something to tell you, as well."

Right. In all the day's happenings, I clean forgot about Dubois coming to see her today. My bad. I needed to make amends first thing.

"Then I expect good news!"

Beside me, Jeff cleared his throat, prompting me to remember what else I needed to tell her. He'd been so quiet after his initial burst of excitement, I'd almost forgotten he was there. But he stood off to one side, as in a trance or a dream. Had he even noticed anything I'd said?

"One more thing before we go, and in case you're wondering, Jeff has promised to cover off some of my duties around here as needed - especially once my real estate business takes off. I hope you're well prepared for him, Jan."

"Long as he stays clear of my kitchen, I'll welcome any and all help."

We waited on a response from him, but he appeared oblivious to anything we'd just said.

"Hello, Jeff? Can you take your mind off the crias for one minute? I need you to reassure Jan that you will fill in for me when I'm busy."

He blinked. "Of course, I'll be here whenever you need me, Jan. Maybe I'll set up a schedule with Frank and Philip to cover me, as well, when needed." He looked at both of us. "Will you excuse me? I should get back to the barn. Mags needs watching. I want to check on the cria. I'll leave Philip there for the first shift. We'll take it in turns until she delivers." He pecked me on the cheek and left.

Jan, with hands-on-hips, had the look that said, *I don't quite believe you Jeff, but we'll manage.*

The day wasn't nearly over, but I didn't think anything could top it.

Just another day down at the farm!

CHAPTER TWENTY-SIX
Dianne

My appetite had finally returned, and I anticipated a delicious supper. I didn't even care if it was a new Cassie dish. I was hungry! I had my car back; suspicion was lifting from me regarding Sloane's murder, and all was right with the world.

Alysha had flown past me a few hours ago, bubbling over with excitement and in a rush to find Jeff. I was eager to hear how her interview had gone.

I sat in the media room, catching up on the news on TV. Normally I avoid it like the plague, but occasionally I thought I should be up to date on what was happening in the world. There's also the good vantage point it offers to see who's coming and going.

Alysha appeared in the doorway. "There you are. I was looking for you."

Before I could say a word, Nina practically skidded to a stop in front of her. "Oh good, you're both here." She held Hemingway in her arms and planted kisses on his head. "We wanted you to know that the vet has given my snookums a clean bill of health!"

I met Alysha's eyes and bit my lip. Too many retorts were vying to escape, so I let Alysha do the talking. "Glad to hear it. Did the vet have any idea what made Hemingway so sick?"

"This naughty little scamp nibbled on bad plants in the garden which could have killed him. Mummy has to keep a much closer eye on you in the future."

"So, as we've said, it's better to let him have his exercise in the run built for him, don't you think?" Alysha kept her tone business-like. "And keep him away from the gardens when he's on a leash."

"One hundred percent agree, chickie. And speaking of walks, we're going to wander down the driveway and have a nice walkie before dinner. Isn't that right, baby?"

With a flourish and leaving behind a scent of something floral and spicy, they were gone. Alysha turned to me, and we both laughed.

"How much longer?"

"Five weeks at the most, but I overheard her saying to Rose she might be cutting her stay short." Alysha held up crossed fingers.

"Hah! I'm with you on that. Now, tell me how your interview went. You were bursting at the seams when you came home earlier."

I was delighted she had done so well. Always a great thrill to start a new chapter. The kid was smart and personable. She'd be a success. I'd have no hesitation recommending her to anyone.

"And you start on Monday? Sounds like we won't be seeing much of you around here for a while."

"Jeff will pick up some of the slack – as long as he remembers. Right now, he's buzzed over the baby alpaca – oops, sorry, cria – and another on the way. I can only hope the novelty will lessen and he focuses on his other responsibilities around here."

"Leave him to me, kiddo. If he gets sidetracked, I'll whip the boy back in line." I flicked an imaginary whip through the air, and she laughed.

"You've got a deal. Now, your turn. Jan told me you have news, which I assume has to do with seeing Dubois today? And I am shamefaced to admit, it didn't dawn on me that your car is back in the driveway!"

"No biggie. You had other things on your mind. As for Dubois. Well, yes, the car is back. But he waffled on confirming whether I'm still under suspicion. He let me know they're investigating Sloane's business accounts. I'm reading between the lines here, but I have a feeling the police have another lead. Dubois also asked whether Rose or I could identify the two who were with Sloane in the Crossings Tavern the day I saw him."

"Did someone say Crossings Tavern?" Cassie stood in the doorway, grocery bags hanging from each arm.

"The day Sloane Jackson showed up when I was in the Tavern with Rose. The police are interested in two other men who were with him that day."

"I saw them, and they were there this afternoon, too. They might even still be there for all I know."

An electric current rushed through me. "You need to talk to the police, Cassie!"

"Sure, I can do that. Once dinner is finished and..."

"Now!" I already had my fingers racing across the keypad on my phone. "May I speak with DC Steven Dubois or Dax Young, please. It's urgent. This is Dianne Mitchell."

Alysha told Cassie to take the groceries to the kitchen, but to come right back. In the meantime, I was connected with Dax. "Yes, Dax. It's concerning Sloane's murder. When DC Dubois was here earlier today, he asked about the two men Sloane had been with. Neither Rose nor I could add information as to the description, but apparently, Cassie can! She says they were there this afternoon and might even still be there."

I finished speaking with him, disconnected the call, and turned to Alysha. Cassie had come back, with Jan trailing behind her. Perfect, I wouldn't have to repeat myself.

"Dubois is off duty, but Dax is on his way here to get a description from Cassie. Sorry, Jan, dinner might be delayed."

"Wouldn't be the first time. I'll put things on hold. Cassie, you stay put here and talk to Dax when he arrives."

I looked at Cassie and Alysha. What a contrast! Cassie's face was a little flushed and her usual nervous energy had skyrocketed. Her fifteen minutes of fame awaited. But Alysha? Her earlier sparkle had evaporated, and her face was clouded.

I was no Kreskin, but I'm pretty sure the change happened when I said Dax was on his way. I'd make it my mission to find out.

CHAPTER TWENTY-SEVEN
Alysha

I didn't know whether to be excited about my new career opportunity and the birth of our new cria or dismayed that Dianne's situation had still not been resolved. And now, for the second time today, I'd need to deal with Dax. I'm grateful to him for the introduction and for kick-starting my real estate career, but the man is so annoying at times.

I tried to relax in our apartment where I waited until Jan let me know he'd arrived. I wasn't anxious to see him again, or was I? Dakotah Young had invaded my dreams more than once lately. Yes, he's attractive and loves to spar with me but his flirting runs hot and cold.

Am I flirting back? Get a grip, Alysha. You love Jeff, don't you?

I left the question unanswered because Jan, using the intercom, informed me her nephew had arrived. Time to get a move on. It was almost dinner time. I hit the bottom step and nearly bumped into Dax. By now I'd learned if he was in uniform, he'd be all *business*. Uniform or not, why did my heart rate pick up a beat whenever he's around?

Not just business mode, but downright somber. No trace of a smile. I thought I'd try to counter the mood. "Hi, Dax. I hope you're bearing good news as it's *only* good news allowed around here today. Thanks again for the introduction to Bennett. I'm starting with him next week."

My attempt at staying upbeat seemed lost on him. There wasn't a lot of enthusiasm when he spoke. "Congratulations. I know you'll be successful working with Bennett. And yes, the birth of a cria - Jan told me. It's all *go* around here, isn't it?"

The small talk over, he got down to business. "I'm here to see Dianne and Cassie. Where might I find them?"

Then I noticed Jan, who had been lingering behind him. She moved forward to answer. "They're waiting for you in the front room. And, Detective, if you have no objection Alysha and I will come, too."

Who flipped his switch? He turned on a megawatt smile. "No objections, ma'am. Lead the way."

As we set foot in the front room, I appreciated the air-conditioned coolness it offered. Cassie wasn't looking so cool, though. She probably would have welcomed a quick toke to calm her nerves. She moved about the room, fussing over plants and coasters as if she couldn't stay still.

Dianne? She was in fine form, sitting in her favourite chair, ready to hold court. She stood as we entered, and cut to the chase, but kept her sense of humour. She wasn't out of the woods yet with the police.

She took the lead. "The gang's all here I see. You'll need to hurry things along, Detective, or run the risk of interfering with our cocktail hour. Can't have our routine disrupted, you know? Unless you have extra handcuffs for the rowdies." She threw him a wink and Jan chuckled.

If Dax bent any lower, he'd leave lip prints on his shiny boots. "My apologies, Dianne. I'll be as quick as I can. Now, I'll start with Cassie." He fished out his notebook. "Ms. Mitchell—Dianne—informed me that you remember seeing the two men with Sloane Jackson the day he confronted her?"

Cassie had finally stopped pacing and stood fixed in place. She nodded.

"I'll take that as a yes," sighed Dax. "How about a description? Did you overhear their names? Any chance you spoke with them?"

Jan moved over to stand with Cassie who looked ready to bolt. "Slow down, Dax. This sounds like an interrogation. You're frightening her."

Dax sat in the nearest chair. "Let's all sit and relax, okay? It's not my intention to frighten you, Cassie, but we're investigating a murder. Any information could be important."

Cassie eyed each of us in turn. I started to think she'd never speak, but then it was verbal diarrhea. Dax scribbled furiously in his notebook, trying to keep up

"They were younger than that man who talked to Dianne. I didn't like him much, either. Oh! But not so much that I'd kill him! Just that he wasn't much of a tipper either. But those other two were trouble. My dad taught me to be on the lookout for their type. So, I always store away any info about the customers in case it's needed. Like right now. They only had a couple of beers when they came in today. But I think they must have had drinks somewhere else because I recognized the signs, you know? They were loaded. Or maybe they were trying to drink to hide from a problem—I don't know. Anyway, one of them, I think he was called Brad, kept pawing at me. And - names. Brad something - he was a total creep! The other didn't talk much. That Brad, though. He was a blabberer!"

I stifled a giggle at her ironic remark and was happy when Dax threw up a hand to make her stop.

"This is terrific, Cassie. You mentioned that they were at the tavern this afternoon. I've sent an officer to have a word - if they're still there."

"Good. I asked my dad - he's working there today - to keep an eye on them before I left. Especially the way one leers at our female customers. The other, I didn't catch a name, keeps more to himself. But neither of them can hold their liquor. And my dad, he worries, you know about drunk drivers. He could lose his liquor licence! They dress like businessmen but no business I'd want to be associated with. They pay with credit cards. Dad would have receipts if you need them."

She leaned back; mouth clamped shut. Had she finally run out of steam?

Dax smiled at her and closed his notebook. "You're beyond observant and helpful. Thank you."

Cassie looked from Jan to Alysha. "Can I go now? I need to work on dinner?"

Dax gave her the go-ahead. "You're free to go. But if you remember anything else - no matter how small - let me know, okay?"

With a vigorous nod of her head, she scampered from the room.

Then he turned to Dianne. "The investigation is ongoing, as I'm sure you're aware, and we anticipate results from the accounting forensics shortly. However, you're still a person of interest. Off the record, Sloane Jackson's associates have moved up the ladder of interest. Other than that, I've nothing concrete to offer, sorry."

He seemed genuinely sorry not to have better news. "You have your car back now. None the worse for wear, I hope?" It seemed a minuscule offering of consolation.

Dianne tapped her fingers against her knees. No detective work needed to see she wasn't happy. "My car is fine. But I expected to hear something positive from you today. Guess beggars can't be choosers, right? To quote you - *I have to hope that if you hear anything, no matter how small, you'll let me know?*"

Dax offered a contrite look but didn't respond. She rose to her feet and continued. "I hope you'll soon get to the bottom of this situation. It's made for an uncomfortable atmosphere around here - for all of us."

Uncomfortable was right. Once again, I felt invisible around Dax and Jan hadn't uttered a word. This was between Dax and Dianne.

"Now, if you don't mind, and with your permission, I'd like to set out the bar cart and try to put some *happy* into our cocktail hour."

Dax had been dismissed, which appeared to be Jan's cue to finally speak. "And I have hungry folks to feed, Dax. So, I'll take my leave if we're done here."

"I appreciate your time, Dianne. And, yes, the minute I have any good news for you, I'll be in touch." Now it was his turn to lighten the mood. "I'll be off then. But perhaps next time the bar cart makes an appearance, I can provide another round of Tequila Sunrise."

In my opinion, I thought he was pushing it, but didn't say anything. Jan had no qualms. "You may be in uniform, but I'm pulling rank as your aunt. Be off with you, and next time we see you, you'd better be telling us you've caught the person responsible for the deaths of Andrew Makwa and Sloane Jackson! Now if you'll excuse me?"

She turned and strode from the room, with Dianne following in her wake. That left me with Dax.

He moved closer to me.

An electric current moved through the room, so intense it could have burned me.

Dax caught my eye. He rubbed the back of his neck and then wouldn't look at me. He mumbled, "Alysha, you must know by now I've feelings for you. And while this is not the time or place, do you think we could talk sometime. Just the two of us?"

I was speechless. When I eventually found my voice, I ignored what he'd said and continued as if I hadn't heard. A childish defense mechanism so I could delay dealing with his revelation.

"I appreciate you dealing with Cassie in such an understanding way. I feared she'd clam up on you when you first started, but you found the best way to ask her questions."

His eyes now scrutinized mine, seeking answers. But I had none and forced myself to remain aloof. "If you're through here, I have a million chores to take care of. Can you see yourself out?" I didn't know how to handle this and anything I said sounded cold and uncaring to my guilty ears.

I took a step away, and he reached for my arm. "I'm sorry, Alysha. I shouldn't have said anything. But I had to, don't you see?" His face registered disbelief, or dashed hopes, at what he'd disclosed to me.

"Just go, Dax. You're still on duty. Perhaps you should attend to *your* business." I couldn't look at him as he moved out of the room, and I sighed with relief when I heard the front door close.

As Dax moved out, I heard the side door close, and I recognized the tune Jeff hummed as he found me. I rearranged couch cushions to avoid looking at him. My discomfort would surely be written all over my face, and I didn't feel in the mood to offer explanations.

"Hi, babe. I see Dax is just leaving. How'd the meeting go? Any update on the murders?"

I couldn't avoid looking at him any longer and came over to kiss him.

"Whoa, babe, not more bad news? You look upset."

"No, sorry. No bad news, although we didn't have much good news either. It's been a roller-coaster day for me, and I guess it's all catching up. What about you? Do we have another alpaca yet?"

I hated it at times when he was so predictable. He clapped his hands together and smiled. "Oh, yes. I've got news on Mags! Philip won't leave her side. Or at least he'll stay in the vicinity, but she's showing all the signs!"

His enthusiasm lifted my spirits, and I put my arms around him for a much-needed hug.

Then he stood back from me. "Hey, are you okay? You look a little pale. Why don't you take the evening off and rest? I'll check in to see you later."

"Stop fussing, I'm good." I tried a small laugh. "I'm not one of your alpacas. I don't need monitoring. The meeting with Dax was fine and things should get sorted out soon. You concentrate on birthing the cria."

I made to move out of his arms. "I'll see you at dinner.

"Don't count on me but I'll try and persuade Philip to eat with everyone. Either way, you'll have a status update on Mags." He was anxious to return to the imminent birth and I didn't stop him.

I stepped out onto the veranda where Dianne, Nina, and Rose were sipping their choice of cocktails while Lily had a soda.

Nina latched on to my presence. "Alysha. We were just wondering what happened with Minnie?"

Dianne gave a small shrug. I took it to mean she hadn't said anything. Once again, I provided a condensed version of events. Minnie, and Frank, were entitled to their privacy, but I confirmed Minnie was doing as well as could be expected. And while she might not be home soon, this would always be her home.

They seemed satisfied with what I had said and offered their wishes that she'd soon be well. I mentally crossed off another item of my never-ending list.

For the next half hour, all seemed right with Leven Lodge's world.

CHAPTER TWENTY-EIGHT
Dianne

Nina and I decided it was high time Alysha had a night off. Being hump-day, Wednesday, it was the perfect time for a mid-week break. The past couple of days had brought highs and lows to the three of us. But especially to Alysha. What with a new job, dealing with Minnie and all the other routine chores she took care of. Jan had been invited as well but had declined. She said she had other commitments, but I suspect it was because Nina was part of the mix. Those two still had no love lost between them.

It was Karaoke night at the Crossings Tavern and if I was willing to make a spectacle of myself, so would Nina and Alysha.

We all needed to have a little fun, and the evil side of me wanted to pull Nina away from her dog-atross called Hemingway. She'd been hesitant to come along, but when Lily volunteered to dog sit, how could she refuse.

And Alysha. Well, something was eating at her, and I suspected that something was Dax. As for me – yeah, enough said.

I drove, Nina rode shotgun and Alysha had the backseat to herself. I'd agreed to fork out for a cab home, if necessary, although I was in no hurry to repeat my last time out with Nina!

For a Wednesday evening, the place was packed. Non-karaoke fans clogged the patio area, but we managed to grab a decent table. We were in luck – $2.00 off all cocktails. I bought the first round. The pub was noisy, but in a good way, and after a couple of sips of my Manhattan, my neck and shoulders relaxed. Nina, an oversized margarita in hand, was loosening up. And Alysha? She seemed to be enjoying her vodka martini. The flush in her cheeks suited her. We had about an hour before the music started. Enough time to get rid of those pesky inhibitions about singing in front of strangers, while still having a chance to vent if needed.

Nina got the ball rolling, with her favourite topic. Her dog. "I don't often leave my precious boy with strangers, but I think he and Lily have bonded!"

"I'd never have seen that coming," said Alysha. "I think she's found something to set her apart from Rose. Cause Rose kinda rules it over her, don't ya think?"

Yes, that martini was a hit with Alysha, and I was happy she was letting her guard down, at least a bit.

Nina chuckled. "You know, I think whoever suggested there might be a story about those two could be on to something. Evil twins have been written to death, so I need a new angle. I'm sure I'll find it. Not at the bottom of this glass, though."

Alysha giggled. "Hey - I really like this martini, but it tastes like more!" She held her empty glass up to the light. "I think, maybe, we should order some fries or something?"

I flagged down a server, ordered fries for sharing and another round. Then I thought I'd test the waters. "Alysha. Can I ask you a question?"

"About real estate?" Her grin was a tiny bit lopsided. "Or alpacas? Just don't ask me about cooking – I know nothing!"

We shared a laugh in common over that, but I wasn't to be sidetracked. I hesitated, briefly, before diving in. I imagined she was still somewhat standoffish with Nina, but I figured after another drink or two we'd all be the best of friends. "Speaking of cooking. What's going on with you and Dax?"

The blush in her cheeks flamed. "There's *nothing* going on. Jeff's my guy. End of story."

"Now, chickie. You'd have to be blind and have one foot in the grave not to notice how he looks at you anytime he comes around." Nina sighed. "Have to say it's been a while since looks like that have come *my* way. What about you, Dianne?" She was smiling, but when the penny dropped, it disappeared. "Oh, sugar. I didn't mean to make you think about Sloane – that piece of trash."

I started on my second Manhattan and blew her off. "Water under the bridge, or should I say body on the road?" Oh, that was bad. A devilish giggle threatened to break loose. "Too soon?"

Nina took the wheel. "Back to Jeff and Dax. A little flirting's good for a gal's ego, but it can turn dangerous way too fast."

Alysha lowered her head. "I'm so confused, but you can't tell anyone. Promise?"

In unison, "We promise."

"I love Jeff with all my heart. I truly do and I never want to hurt him. But Dax – well, he gets to me, you know?"

"Gets the juices flowing like Jeff can't, am I right, chickie?"

Indignation flashed across Alysha's face at the assumption. "We haven't done anything! He just flirts with me, that's all. And then other times, he's like a fricking ice machine."

Nina was pushing the wrong buttons with Alysha, and I didn't want the evening to blow up in our faces. "Kiddo, calm down. It's obvious he gets under your skin. But you need to nip it in the bud – unless you want something to happen?"

"No, I don't. I don't think so. Oh, damn – I just don't know. Period!"

Nina and I shared a look of commiseration, also known as experience.

"Listen, Alysha. You and you alone are responsible for how you react. I think at times, we all get a little bored with our usual lives and the lure of a little excitement can be tempting. And that's all I'm gonna say on that because I'm not exactly a role model for healthy relationships."

"And just because you're so cute and have put up with my darling Hemingway this past week, I'll offer my advice, chickie."

I trained my eyes on Alysha, ready to shut Nina down if she crossed any lines.

"And your advice is?" Alysha's tone was cool.

"I may not know you very well, and Jeff, well hardly at all. But what I have seen of the two of you together makes me think you have something special, and I'd think twice, no three times, before risking that." She drained her glass and signaled a passing server for another. "But for now – let's sing!"

Perfect timing. The mic was being set up and eager participants, fueled on by alcohol, were perusing song choices. I wondered if they'd have any Gordon Lightfoot?

***

We truly had a great evening. It felt so good to laugh and be silly. Alysha ventured up for a couple of songs. I got lost with *Carefree Highway* and *Cotton Jenny*. Nina wasn't shy at all, and we finished off the evening as a trio singing *Dancing Queen*. I'm sure the applause was genuine!

The evening was warm, and we decided to go for a coffee before heading home. I felt I was fine to drive. I'd been a good girl, only two cocktails and lots of water. We left the coffee shop, still lighthearted and reliving highlights of the evening.

There weren't too many people about. The bars wouldn't be emptying for another hour or so. We linked arms and crossed over a side street when the sound of crashing garbage cans echoing off a building's brick wall stopped us. The lighting was dim, but I made out a figure struggling to stand, next to a dumpster.

I yelled out, "Hey, are you alright?" And then recognition. The kid who had tried to steal Nina's car. "Nina – it's him!"

She was quick on the uptake; I'll grant her that. We both took off at a fast clip, leaving Alysha in our dust. The kid must have been stunned when he crashed into the metal cans because he seemed in a daze and unable to comprehend why two women, in heels, were running toward him, and not away!

He lost valuable seconds trying to upright a bicycle, which was to our advantage. Nina got to him first and grabbed him by the collar. "You little prick! Do you know what a new paint job is going to cost me?"

She was about to knee him when I halted her. "Whoa! You don't need an assault charge." She still gripped his collar, and I shoved his bike out of the way and then grabbed one of his arms.

By this time, Alysha had caught up, waving her cell phone. "I'll call the cops!"

"No! Don't. Please? *Please!*" He was wild-eyed, and nearly in tears. He tried to shake his arm loose from my hold. And then he deflated. "Please."

Alysha's finger was poised over her phone, but she looked to Nina and me for permission. I relented. "Put the phone down, for now."

Tears streamed down our captive's face and then I had a good look at him. Was he even sixteen? I'm not much for maternal feelings, but something about this kid tugged at my heart. He was scared shitless. More of the cops than us. Probably didn't want his parents to know. Or was there something else?

"Nina, let go. Let's hear what junior has to say to us."

She unclenched her hand from his shirt but didn't move away. Ready in an instant to grapple with him. As was I. But I'd give him a chance to talk.

"What's your name?"

"C-Cory."

"Cory what?" demanded Nina.

Alysha interrupted. "Guys. I think we should call the cops. Or his parents." And then she glanced back over her shoulder to see if anyone was watching.

"Trust me, chickie, if Cory here doesn't have a good story, I'll call them myself."

Cory wiped at his eyes. "It's Cory Banker. My parents won't care. I ran away a year ago." He gulped air. "If the cops come, I'll have to tell them what I saw. Then I'll be dead meat."

Hey now, this sounded interesting. "Go on. We're listening."

"Those killers. They know I saw them."

Chills raced up my spine. I swallowed, and before I asked, I knew. "Sloane Jackson?"

Cory nodded, his lips quivering. "If that's the guy from River Road, yes."

Nina stepped up to the plate. I'd gone numb processing the revelation. She spoke to him, but not unkindly. "We have to call the cops, kid. Otherwise, we'll be accessories after the fact or something."

Alysha moved a little closer to Cory. "Listen, I know the Detective handling the case and I can trust him. I guarantee he'll keep you safe. Safer than being out on the streets."

Nina put a hand over Alysha's cell. "I agree we have to call, but let's hear his story first. And then call."

I tried to gather my wits. "Besides," I argued, "the more people who know Cory's story, the safer he'll be."

Alysha gave me a mystified look. "And pray tell, Dianne, how do you figure that?"

I hadn't thought it through and could only shrug my shoulders. "A theory? Listen, give him five minutes to at least start the story and then call Dax. Okay?"

She was irked, her face like stone. "And I suppose, Nina, you're looking for story ideas and you'd like to hear the grizzly details as well?"

Nina tried a smile of surrender. "What can I say, sunshine?"

"I'm not happy about this. Five minutes. Start talking, Cory."

The kid looked green, and I worried he was going to throw up. "You heard her. What happened?"

"It started with the well."

"Well, what?" I asked. What was I missing?

"No, I mean *a* well. Drinking water, you know. Over by the new restaurant spa place."

Suddenly, Alysha seemed fine with hearing the story. Anything to do with her family history got her attention. And the old mill property hadn't been her favourite place last year. "You mean by the old mill? Where the new resort is?"

"Yeah, I guess. Anyway, I was taking a shortcut that night and saw a guy talking with two men. Near the well for the place. He might have been older than me, but they were arguing. He pushed at one of the men and the creep sucker-punched him. The kid fell down and the other guy..."

The colour drained from his face, and we waited for him. "The other guy picked up a rock and bashed his head. That's when I ran. They didn't see me. That time."

Alysha kept glancing at her watch. She was getting nervous, and I knew she wanted to call the cops, but I needed to hear more. Especially if it concerned Sloane. "And Sloane Jackson? River Road?"

"Right. I'd seen him around town. Flashy guy. Figured I could follow him, see where he lived. Break in, grab some stuff to get cash. My plan was to go back, watch the place and break in the next time he left."

The more Cory talked, the less frightened he seemed. Like he was talking about somebody else. I knew how that felt. A survival mechanism. No one interrupted him and he continued.

"My plan went to shit when I showed up to see him in a huge fight with the same two guys I'd seen at the mill that night. It's an isolated place, right? And they were out in the driveway. Everyone was shouting. Mad at each other. I hid behind a tree across the street so I couldn't catch what they were saying. It looked like one of them pulled a gun on the Jackson guy."

The kid had all our attention. I couldn't explain the emotions going through me. I had put Sloane out of my life, but I never wanted to see him dead - murdered. Listening to how his final moments ended up made me want to cry. None of us spoke. Cory wasn't done yet.

"I thought for sure they'd shoot him, you know? And it happened so fast. The guy holding the gun hit Jackson across the head with it and he fell. I must have made a noise 'cause both of them looked right where I was. I didn't wait around, but they saw me when I ran. And your car, lady - I needed to get out of town and it would have been a sweet ride. Sorry about the scratches."

Now he was done and shaking like a leaf. I had no words. On some level, I knew I'd be cleared of killing Sloane, but I felt detached from the whole scene. Alysha's voice penetrated my brain fog. "I'm calling the cops."

We'd all been so riveted on hearing Cory's tale, we'd never become aware we had company until an ice-cold voice said, "Put the phone down, or you're all dead."

CHAPTER TWENTY-NINE
Alysha

Blame it on the alcohol slowing my reaction time. I continued the call. Three numbers. Just three numbers. I barely heard "Emergency, how..." when my phone was ripped from my hand.

Adrenaline pushed through the sluggishness brought on by the martinis I'd enjoyed. I'm not a big drinker, but it had been a fun, and relaxing, evening. Until now.

I dropped my hands to my sides and swiveled around. Cory stood stock-still, with a gun pointed at his head. The hand holding the gun didn't look steady.

Then Dianne shrieked. "Nina!"

Nina had made a run for it. She didn't get far. A shot rang out and she fell between two dumpsters.

I screamed and took a step until my arm was yanked back by the shooter. He brandished the gun in my face. "Move! Over there with the others."

Dianne and Cory stood against the brick wall. She had a protective arm around the kid. I ran to join them. She and I exchanged glances. I prayed my call had reached someone and help was on the way. Or surely someone had heard the gunshot?

I assumed one of these guys was Brad, whom Cassie had identified. She'd pegged him as a talker, so I figured the one who'd grabbed me was Brad. He seemed more talkative and nervous than his counterpart.

Dianne put on a brave front and addressed the calmer of the two. "I need to see how my friend is."

"Go ahead, lady. My friend can put a bullet in you as well. Want to try?"

She shrank back against the wall.

A manic laugh came from Brad. "That'd be fine with me. I like the sound it makes when I shoot. What do you say, Derek? No witnesses, right?"

Derek cuffed Brad across the head. "Idiot," he hissed. "No names, you stupid screw-up." He wiped his hand across his mouth. "Let me think. Cops will be on the way by now."

Cory, sandwiched between Dianne and me, trembled. He pleaded with our captives. "Please. I won't say anything. They won't either, right?"

I could only nod like a puppet. Dianne looked ready to heave. And poor Cory. So scared he wet himself. Where were the cops! There'd be no Jeff coming to the rescue this time.

In the distance, at last, sirens! Derek had come to a decision, and Brad shifted his gun back and forth in front of us. "Shit. One body tonight's enough. Grab the kid. He can be insurance."

"Oh, ya, right. Like a bargaining chip. I like it."

"I don't care if you like it. Get him. As for you two. It's your lucky day. I'm not a murderer, but I can't say the same about my friend here."

Cory yelped as Brad snatched him from between us. The sirens grew louder. Dianne and I stood paralyzed and watched helplessly as the three figures faded into the darkness.

Slamming car doors sparked us into action and we ran to the dumpster.

Nina lay on her side, motionless. I touched her. "Oh my god. Nina!"

Dianne rolled Nina onto her back, grimacing at the blood oozing from her shoulder. When Nina opened her eyes, we both jumped. "Took you long enough, chickies. I've been playing dead on this cold ground, waiting for you. Great research for the book, though."

I laughed in relief, as voices came closer. "Then you'll be glad to know the cavalry's here."

Dianne sat down beside Nina. I turned to face several policemen advancing on us, guns drawn. Someone in charge soon assessed guns weren't necessary and weapons returned to holsters.

"We need an ambulance," was all I could think to say.

***

Dianne looked as exhausted as I felt, and I'd sobered up lightning fast. We were both fixated on the cubicle in the emergency department where they'd taken Nina.

We waved off doctors who wanted to examine us. Dax and a couple of other officers milled around waiting, like us, for a verdict on our resident writer.

I held on to Dianne's hand, which occasionally trembled. Delayed shock? Maybe she should see a doctor after all.

The thought flew away as the entrance to the emergency department swung open, and I saw my guy.

Jeff's face was stricken with fear, but when I rushed into his arms, he could see that I was alright.

After a lengthy hug and warm kiss, he pulled back to look at me. "Oh Aly, if anything had happened to you... You are okay, right?"

"Babe, I'm fine. It's Nina who was hurt. We're waiting for word. How did you find out?"

"Dax called me. What happened? You're sure you're not hurt?" And like an afterthought, "Dianne! You're okay too?"

The questions came fast and furious. The concern in his voice made me feel guilty. I'd caused him worry about my safety. Again.

Before I could offer words of reassurance, the cubicle curtains parted. A doctor emerged. He was followed by Nina, who wore a sling and a face-splitting grin. "A welcoming committee. Splendid, just splendid." She turned to the doctor and thanked him, profusely, for his care. "And now I must get home. My precious will be so upset wondering where his mummy is."

I bit my lip at the expression on the doctor's face. He composed himself and handed Nina instructions for her wound care. "She should be fine. Rest is important for a day or two. Goodnight."

Nina moved toward Jeff's outstretched arm as he said, "If I may do the honours? Your chariot awaits."

I suspected Ms. Mikado was a little shitfaced. The doc had given her something for the pain, but I wasn't in the mood to be her nurse. I sighed to myself. But if not me, then it would likely be Jan. Maybe we'd toss a coin when we got home. And I was concerned about Dianne as well. She might not have been hurt, but I could see lengthy recap discussions on the horizon.

I called out to Jeff as he maneuvered Nina through the out-patient doors. "Thanks for taking her. Dianne and I will be right behind you - we still have to talk to the police and then we'll be straight home."

I helped Dianne to her feet and glanced over at Dax. He walked over to us and avoided looking at me. Now what had I done? He asked if there was anything else we needed.

Dianne answered him." Thank you. I think we just need to get home and I need to soak in a tub. I've had enough excitement for one day."

"I'm glad you're both none the worse for wear. You've both had a close call this evening. I have your basic statements for now and will come by tomorrow if I need more."

I knew it was too good to be true. Dianne might be longing for a tub soak, but she was also craving information. I could see the questions ramping full speed. Talk about a second wind!

"But what happened to those guys? You got them, right? Or did they get away? Do you think they murdered Sloane? And that poor boy. I hope he's okay. He's a bit misguided and seems like a lost soul."

In spite of himself, Dax laughed. "Slow down there. Here's what I can tell you. We have the shooter, and his accomplice, in custody. Cory will get the help he needs. He's like so many youths I've worked with.

Lack of guidance and not enough positive influence. With luck, he'll be okay. I think we may have saved him in time - he's had a frightening brush with the wrong side of the law. When I have anything further to add, you'll be the first to know. Deal?"

Dianne nodded and looked relieved. "Right, thanks. And can I get a ride back to pick up my car?"

"Your car will be fine downtown, Dianne, and can be picked up tomorrow. I'll have one of the patrol guys keep an eye on it."

He finally acknowledged me. "You've both had a big shock this evening and there'll be no driving for either of you." He crooked a finger at one of his constables. "Here's your driver for tonight. He'll get you home."

I hoped the car would be warmer than the chill enveloping me. Well, two could play that frosty game. "Thank you and goodnight, Dax."

CHAPTER THIRTY
Dianne

The place was buzzing. There'd be no way to keep all of last night's excitement from my housemates. Breakfast had grown cold while Alysha recounted the events. Nina was in her glory - re-enacting her failed escape from her would-be murderer. Her clipped wing didn't slow her down at all. Lily had been quick to volunteer to take Hemingway for walks if it was too much for Nina. But I don't think Nina appreciated being interrupted during her murder attempt scene. She nodded her acceptance to the offer and carried on with her account.

We had a captive audience. Rose and Lily had been open-mouthed, and Philip hadn't even peeked at his latest book. Should I admit I was disappointed Minnie wasn't here with her sharp retorts?

Jeff kept touching Alysha's hand as if to ensure she hadn't been harmed.

I hadn't contributed much; it was easier to let Alysha and Nina share the spotlight. I'd only be happy if everything finally led to my name being cleared of any wrongdoing where Sloane was concerned.

And I kept thinking about the kid, Cory. Cory Jerome Banker was his full name according to the police. Something about him had affected me. I hoped he'd survive this situation in one piece. He was barely sixteen. This kind of stuff on his record would do a number on his future. My musings were cut short when our attention was drawn to a commotion in the kitchen.

Frank burst into the dining room. "Jeff. It's happening now. You and Philip don't want to miss our second cria, do you?"

Jeff scraped his chair back. "Aly?"

She laughed. "Get. I'll come down to the barn in a bit. The police are supposed to be here before noon, so I need to stick around. Good luck!"

He planted a kiss on the top of her head and dashed off with Frank. Philip right behind them. Funny thing with men. How they bond over things like cars or alpacas, and that's all they can focus on.

She turned her focus to the rest of us at the table. "So, that's two names we have to come up with. How about we all think of some ideas for the two little ones?"

"Sounds like fun," said Lily. "How will we decide though?"

Jan came in from the kitchen with a bowl, pens, and slips of paper. "Put your suggestions down, then names can be drawn from the bowl." She also handed out six pieces of paper – one for each of us. "Each name you like gets a point. Add up the points. Top two names win out."

"And you suggest some names as well, Jan," said Alysha. "This is a great idea, thanks!"

"No, ladies, but thank you. This is your job for the morning. I'll concentrate on the chores."

Jan was in mother mode. Keeping the children busy. She did that with no effort. It was a trait I admired.

For the next hour, we scribbled and giggled our way through names. When our efforts were exhausted, Alysha decreed a short break. "Besides, the men should be here for this. We've kind of hijacked the naming thing and I don't want them to feel left out."

"Can't have men with hurt feelings, can we, sunshine?" Nina said. The comment was met with knowledgeable smiles of agreement.

"Alysha. Sorry to interrupt the fun, but the police are here. Dax, and Dubois, are waiting for you across the hall. For Nina and Dianne as well." Jan picked up on the twins' eager faces. "And I'd strongly suggest you two make yourselves scarce. Understood?"

With reluctance, our table companions left the dining room. Then the three of us went into the front room. Dax and Dubois, when out of uniform, appeared less intimidating. My antenna was on Alysha. She made sure she was as far away from Jan's nephew as possible.

Dax's face was unreadable, but Dubois looked...happy? Especially when he turned those blue eyes on me. Be still my heart. Or was it hammering because I anticipated good news, for me?

Dax held a sheaf of papers in his hands. "Let's sit. We've lots to cover."

And oh, boy, he didn't even look at her.

Trust Nina to liven up the proceedings. "I miss the uniforms, boys. Although you both clean up pretty sweet in civvies." She was in fine form, perhaps with a little assistance from pain medication.

Dax didn't take the bait but stayed professional. "How's the shoulder today, Ms. Mikado?"

"Just a flesh wound, officer. Oh, do you know how long I've wanted to say that?" She giggled.

No tequila for her today.

Alysha didn't appear in the mood and cut to the chase. "Can we get to it? I'm anxious to be with Jeff. He's overseeing the birth of another cria, right now."

"Of course." Then Dax turned to me. "Let's start with you. I'm sure you'll be relieved to know you are no longer a person of interest in Sloane Jackson's murder. Brady Crockett has been charged with his death, along with the death of Andrew Makwa. His associate, Derek Hutcheson is being charged as an accessory after the fact. They are in court this morning for arraignment."

Part of me wanted to gush my thanks, but there was enough of that from Nina's quarter, so I tried to be mature. "Yes, very relieved. Thank you. Thank you."

Alysha came over to me and hugged me. "I'm so relieved for you as well. I knew you hadn't done anything wrong." She sent the next barb Dax's way. "I told you she was innocent!"

Dax wouldn't respond and flipped through more pages. "Here's what I'm at liberty to tell you, for now. Hutcheson and Crocket were business associates with Sloane Jackson. He could have made a better choice. They don't have a reputation for honest dealings but had the ready cash Jackson needed for the Rivermill investment. Accounting forensics has shown us a lot of inconsistencies with their books, which Jackson must have discovered as well. Likely the source of the confrontation Cory witnessed."

Sloane may have been a lot of things, but I'd vouch for his business integrity any day. He'd had a greedy streak, though. Probably his Achilles heel with his so-called partners. Shoot, Dax was still talking, and I needed to focus. There was something I wanted to discuss with him after he was done. Alone.

"...and Hutcheson seemed only too eager to throw Crockett under the bus. We're waiting on forensics for proof, but according to Hutcheson, Crockett killed Andrew Makwa when Andrew discovered him about to pour a substance into the well which supplies the drinking water for the Rivermill facility, as well as several other homes in the area."

We hadn't noticed Jan standing beside the door frame. Her hand flew to her mouth, and she gasped. "But the police said drugs were involved. Is that incorrect? Dax? Answer me."

He stood and moved over to his aunt. Placing a hand on her shoulder he spoke in a tone of voice that conveyed love and concern. "We've already let Andrew's family know he'd done nothing wrong. While we did find evidence of drug use near his body, it's since been dismissed as having any connection with his death. A bad, bad coincidence."

Jan's face brightened. "I'm so happy to hear this. Thank you. And you, as well, Steven. You've earned your pay this month." Then she looked at all of us. "I'm sorry, I didn't mean to intrude, but I had to know. I'll be out of your way now. Time to call my parents and give them the news as well."

Nina had grown quiet. I nudged Alysha to look. The meds had caused our writing diva to nod off. We let her be.

"Dax. Can I ask about the Rivermill property? Can it reopen? And even more important, was the well contaminated?" Alysha may have addressed Dax, but she barely looked at him.

"As far as the facility goes, our investigation is complete. You'll be happy to know Jackson and his cohorts weren't the only investors. So, the business should resume. But I believe the Board of Health will continue testing the water to see if further action is needed. I suggest you contact them for updates, although the last I heard they had said the water was potable."

"Fine," she said. "I'll be sure to do so later today. But now, I need to go and see what's happening with our alpacas. Thanks for coming by with the update."

Wow, the tension between those two was thick! He watched her as she left, and then turned to me. "You wanted a word?"

I looked at sleeping beauty. "Can we talk outside?"

Dubois took his cue. "If you're going to be a few minutes, I wouldn't mind having a peek at the alpacas? Okay with you, Dax?"

Dax laughed. "Go ahead, you old softie. I know where to find you."

Nina was out cold, and we could have probably talked in front of her, but I wanted some space and fresh air.

I walked with him toward a bench away from the veranda and inquisitive ears. I had no desire to beat about the bush and came straight to the point. "It's about the kid, Cory. What's going to happen to him?"

Dax gave me a puzzled look. "You were concerned about him last night as well. Why?"

I wasn't sure how to answer because I really didn't know either. "I don't know. Something about him. Last night he was so scared. Will he go back to his parents?"

"Listen, Dianne. Cory has had a couple of minor infractions. His home life was terrible, and he's been living on the streets since he was about fourteen. He's under seventeen so he qualifies for Protections Services and possibly foster care."

I nodded, taking it all in, and before thoughts even formed, words spilled. "Can I help him, somehow? I know I can't foster him here, but I'd like to be involved with him. Provide him with opportunities he might not otherwise have. Too many kids get short-changed. I'd...I'd like to make a difference in one life if I can? And I'm sure I can get Nina to drop any car theft charges."

The warmth in his eyes was natural. "You're a woman after my own heart. I see too much with kids on the reserve and everywhere. Lives that miss out on potential because no one cares. I'll make some inquiries. Maybe a social worker will be in touch. Kids like Cory need a mentor and to know someone genuinely cares. Thank you."

I wasn't quite sure what I'd just done, but it felt right. "Okay then. I'll be expecting a call. Soon. Promise?"

"I promise."

Jan came bounding down the veranda steps. "Is Alysha here? A potential new resident is on the phone! I thought she'd have her phone with her, but it went to voicemail."

"Pretty sure she's watching another birth. Out in the field," said Dax. "Listen, I need to corral my partner anyway, so I'll go and tell her. It might be best if you took a message. She'll call them back?" He took his leave, and I heard him say under his breath. "I need to clear the air with her once and for all."

CHAPTER THIRTY-ONE
Alysha

Arriving at the barn I followed the excited but subdued voices of the men, who were further out in the pasture. Jeff, Frank, Philip, and now Dubois were gazing with reverence at the spectacle of Mags delivering her first cria.

I ran over to stand by Jeff. "Oh Jeff, she's beautiful." I too gazed at this splendid creature. Jet black and already looking for her mama.

Jeff took my hand and pulled me to him. "Not sure of the sex yet but yes, beautiful."

He turned me around away from the others. His face, so earnest searched mine. "Aly, I.. I know you get tired of hearing me talk alpacas all the time, but this is what I'm meant to do. I love everything about this life, especially the breeding."

"What? Even more than computer programs?" He'd grown so serious I wanted to have a chance to catch up to his mood.

"Yes, even computers. But seriously, no matter what happens to you and I.. Oh, that didn't come out right. What I mean to say is I promise to help you all I can with the lodge, but I need to know I can continue working to expand the herd. You've said you need time for your real estate business. Well, I need time for my business as well."

It was true. Had I been too one-sided in our relationship? I guess I'd been demanding about my work needs, without realizing the alpacas had become Jeff's business world as well. Equally demanding of his time.

"Guys, look!" whispered Frank.

We turned back to see Mags nudging her baby to its feet. I gave Frank a two-thumbs-up and centered my attention back to Jeff. "Jeff, look at me."

He wore a bewildered look on his face as if I was going to tell him he'd been a naughty boy and he couldn't get his way.

"I love you and together we'll make this work. You with the alpacas and me with my real estate dreams. We'll support each other and still manage the Lodge. With extra help if need be. Okay?"

Jeff took me in his arms and kissed me. I reveled in the closeness we were sharing when I heard Dax's voice call my name. Damn, how to spoil a mood.

We broke our embrace and turned to see Dax.

Jeff admonished him. "You need to keep your voice down. Mags has just given birth. We'll try not to bother her while she adjusts to motherhood.

Dax nodded and lowered his voice. "Sorry. Not my area of expertise, you know."

Satisfied Dax would behave, Jeff left my side and went back to his charges.

No one was left to act as a buffer between us. I worked to keep my voice level. "You wanted to speak to me?"

"Yes, I do but before I forget, Jan says you have a call about a potential resident for the lodge. She tried to call you, but no answer. I suggested she tell them you'll call back?"

I kept my business face on. "She'll need to take a message." I pulled my phone out from my back pocket and sent Jan a text of apology.

"Jan's taken care of. What else? Maybe you can tell me what's on your mind and I can get on with managing my business."

The smile on his face wavered and his voice held no hint of ego. "Can we meet somewhere - more private - to talk so that I can explain? Maybe this evening?"

My chest tightened. Instinct said I didn't want to hear anything he had to say or explain. "No Dax, we can't. See that?" I pointed over to the pasture, where Jeff and his buddies still concentrated on the recent arrival. They were like big kids in their excitement over Mags and her newborn. "We've had a load of excitement here the last few days with the birth of the crias, among other things, and my place is here, to support Jeff."

Dax looked forlorn. *Low blow Alysha*. "So, if you've something to say, you'd better say it here and now."

Forlorn and now uncomfortable, not his usual overconfident self. No bluster to his voice, more like resignation. "I came to see for myself the - crias - is that what you call them? And drag Dubois away. He'll be telling the story all over the station before the end of the day."

I was confident that wasn't the only reason he wanted to see me, but I didn't feel like making this easy on him. I waited.

"But if you won't meet me... I'd better spit it out."

I had a sense of where this was heading, and for my own protection knew I had to *stand fast*. "Listen, Dax. I'm sorry, but I don't have all day. What is it? What did you want to say to me?"

"Alysha, I know I've made you uncomfortable with my obvious flirting and declaration of how I feel about you."

This was torture and I wanted it to end. He had more on his mind, and I didn't interrupt. Just wanted to get it over with. I didn't know what to say that wouldn't make me sound like an idiot anyway.

"But, in all honesty, I can see how much you and Jeff are suited to one another. You were meant to be together."

He looked over at Jeff, who was busy preparing to move Mags and her cria to the barn when she was ready. Dubois waved at us to join them.

"He's one lucky guy and I wish you both..." His voice trailed off and he mumbled, "I won't be bothering you anymore. I've accepted a promotion as an Inspector with Toronto Police Services. I'll wrap up the murder case here and then I'll transfer."

I hadn't expected that kind of news and I couldn't look at him until I had the semblance of a smile on my face. A smile that hurt in my effort to hold back tears. A part of me would always be attracted to him. And maybe in another time and place... Well, that was useless thinking. Better not to let on. Easier on both of us that way.

"Congratulations, Dax, I'm happy for you and the new position. Well deserved. Does Jan know?"

"Yes, I told her just now. She's pleased for me but feels I'm letting our people down. Then I told her our people are everywhere and some are living miserable lives in Toronto. Maybe I'll be in a position to help more."

"You're a good man, Dakotah Young. Jan, and I, will be very proud of you. For now, though, I can't thank you enough for so many things you've helped with. Clearing Dianne's name, and the introduction to Bennett. Oh," I laughed to lighten the mood. "How could I forget our barman extraordinaire with amazing Tequila Sunrises?" I paused and risked a sentimental comment. "And, for making me realize just how much I do love Jeff. I believe in our future together, and have confidence you *will* find someone who makes you as happy as I am."

Dax managed a smile. "I'll never forget you, Alysha. But maybe we shouldn't hug, as much as I would like to. I need to get Dubois out of here and back to his real job before he decides to become a farmer."

I didn't think Jeff or Frank would appreciate the farmer comment and let it go. Or maybe Dax didn't mean it to sound derogatory. Must be me.

We joined the guys and after admiring the cria I left them to go back to the house and attend to my business. I turned and walked away. I needed a distraction.

***

And distractions I found. Jan was anxious to give me several messages. A couple, Mr. and Mrs. Patel, were interested in a long-term stay with us. I needed to call them back and discuss the details. I had a good feeling the McTaggarts' room wouldn't be empty much longer.

Then Nina! She wanted to see Jan and me about staying on until Christmas! We told her we'd think about it and let her know before the end of the day. I had to reluctantly admit she'd livened up the place. There'd need to be boundaries and it would depend a lot on Jan.

Bennett Howes had also called for me. Something about a new rural property coming available and it would be ideal for me to use as my first listing!

I grabbed a coffee and stepped out onto the veranda. Pitchers of iced tea and cucumber water sat next to a plate of homemade cookies. My *family* were all there. Philip, reading up on the care of young alpacas. Rose and Lily playing cards. Dianne, who'd had a call from Social Services, was leafing through catalogues. She'd told me Cory Banker was in dire need of new clothes.

Lost in thought, I hadn't heard Jan come up beside me. She held two slips of papers which I recognized. "Alysha. The boys have approved the names for their new babies. Roxy for the female cria and Ryker for the male. They were the most popular choices. What do you think?"

"If that's why the guys like, who am I to say otherwise?" I winked at her.

Jeff and I had an exciting and wonderful future ahead of us. Leven Lodge was truly home. But right now, I needed to book that couples' massage.

THE END

Who is Jamie Tremain?

Jamie Tremain was "born" in the summer of 2007. A collaborative effort brought about by two fledgling authors **Liz Lindsay and Pam Blance**. Pam and Liz met at their place of work and once a mutual interest in reading (and writing!) was discovered, there was no stopping them! To date Jamie Tremain has published the Dorothy Dennehy Mystery Series and has now released the first book in a new Grant's Crossing Series – Death on the Alder

Even before their first book, The Silk Shroud, was published, they had been actively building their brand. One of their fortes was, and still is, interviews on their blog with other authors – and readers. Networking within the supportive writing community continues to be a priority. A recent "Author Survival Network" private group was established on Facebook, to offer fellow authors a place to meet, share experiences and offer encouragement to each other.

Jamie Tremain belongs to Crime Writers of Canada, International Thriller Writers, and are proud to be part of the Genre5 Writers group in Guelph, Ontario.

Follow us at https://jamietremain.blogspot.com/ or http://www.jamietremain.ca/

Books by Jamie Tremain
The Dorothy Dennehy Mystery Series

- The Silk Shroud
- Lightning Strike
- Beholden to None

The Grant's Crossing Series

- Death on the Alder
- Resort to Murder
- Coming soon – *Theatre of Foul Play* (tentative title)

Don't miss out!

Visit the website below and you can sign up to receive emails whenever Jamie Tremain publishes a new book. There's no charge and no obligation.

https://books2read.com/r/B-A-VAAO-JRVUB

BOOKS 2 READ

Connecting independent readers to independent writers.

Lightning Source UK Ltd.
Milton Keynes UK
UKHW040757070222
398308UK00001B/179

9 798201 262426